Albatross
(The Curse of Honesty)

Robert Nichols

Mountain Muse Publishing
Lincoln City, Oregon

Mountain Muse Publishing Company

ISBN 978-0-9627615-3-9 (UPUB)
ISBN 978-0-9627615-4-6 (Kindle)
ISBN 978-0-9980910-3-7 (Paperback)
Electronic Fiction/Print Fiction
©2001 Robert Nichols
All rights reserved
Electronic Publication ©2013
Paperback Publication ©2018
Requests for information should be addressed to:

Robert Nichols
Box 406
Lincoln City, OR 97367
MtMuse44@aol.com

MtMusePublishing.com

Cover design and typesetting: Robert Nichols

Table of Contents

Dedication

Dedicated to the mystery,
the farce,
the essential wonder
of love.

Definitions:

Bullshit: 1. The exaggeration, distortion, or concoction of words, ideas, actions, or concepts for relatively innocuous purposes relating to social intercourse and self-deception—not to be confused with blatant dishonesty (used car salesmen and lovers are bullshiters; radio/TV evangelists and politicians are liars). 2. The half-truths that inflate the illusion of reality. 3. White lies, cow pies and alibis. 4. Sometimes, just about everything in the world except fear.

Mish Kia: The little known and rarely practiced Japanese martial art of meat cleaving.

About *Albatross*

This was my first novel (of three, so far). I finished the first draft while living in a roach-infested one-room apartment in downtown Denver. That was the summer of 1974. Over the years I have been fooling with the original text right up to today. It is still pretty much the same story. I think I'll hit the publish button on this version today. Enjoy.

Robert Nichols / September 19, 2018

**"It is an ancient mariner
and he stoppeth one..."**

Hello.

I'll call you Newfriend.

This won't take very long, an hour or so and then you'll be free to leave. I'm sorry I don't have furniture, but the rug is thick—it might almost be comfortable.

I won't be needing you for long. Just a short time and you can go on to be an honored guest at your cousin's or niece's or whoever's wedding party you were heading for when I captured you.

Sit down, lie down, curl into a fetal ball–whatever, and, while we wait, I'll say what I need to say. Just stay here and wait with me.

And, please, listen.

It was way up in northern North Dakota where horizons are faint lines drawn between dirt fields and sky fields, and roads are scarce and wind-crossed. I was a hitchhiker, a fisherman with a thumb-line cast to an empty sea.

I was standing beside a two-lane highway and there were few cars and few people. A farmer had let me off late in the afternoon and then turned off on a dirt road reaching to the northern horizon. For a long time, I stood there watching the cloud of dust rising from behind his fast departing car until it finally disappeared beyond the edge of the world.

Sometimes twenty-five or thirty minutes would pass between cars, maybe longer, and then, when darkness came, much longer.

I didn't care.

I took out my harmonica and played "Oh, Shenandoah."

It was a ten-thousand-starred night, perfectly still save for an occasional small gust of wind and my slurring harmonica sounds.

Across the vast face of the planet, I was alone. I didn't care. I was nineteen.

As I played I thought, my song is filling the whole Universe and nobody can hear it. Nobody at all.

It didn't matter. It was fifteen years ago, and I thought it didn't matter.

I was wrong.

You see, I'm alone again and, even here in this lush land and living deeply within this amiable town of dear hearts and gentle people, the landscape is just as desolate, and still nobody is hearing my song, my story. And, yes, it really matters. In the distant vacancy of North Dakota, a naive boy had been a fool; and now, in the distant vacancy of this town full of friends and loved ones, a man is desperate.

That's the reason I stopped you down there on the sidewalk and lured you up here to this hollow apartment with my "glittering eye."

Do you know "The Rime of the Ancient Mariner?"

I know I'm nuts. Don't worry about it. I'm probably harmless anyway.   Listen:

It is an ancient Mariner,
And he stoppeth one of three.
"By thy long grey beard and glittering eye,
Now wherefore stopp'st thou me?

The bridegroom's doors are opened wide,
And I am next of kin;
The guests are met, the feast is set:
May'st hear the merry din."

He holds him with his glittering eye--
The Wedding-guest stood still,

And listens like a three-years' child:
The Mariner hath his will.

Do you get it? "Glittering eye..." It's me, I'm thirty-four years old and, already, I'm an "Ancient Mariner"—not quite so gray maybe, but it's true. Do you know the story he tells? What? A little hazy, you say? Jeez, you must have slept right thorough English literature class. Stay awake this time, Newfriend. Listen.

The ancient mariner was a sailor sailing away on a good ship, the wind was blowing the right direction, the weather was perfect, everything was just fine. And then, for no apparent reason, he took a little target practice with his handy crossbow and shot down a bird that had been flying along with the ship and bringing it all the good luck. An albatross. From that point on, everything went to hell— he had ruined all the good luck with that thoughtless bit of archery. The dead albatross hung around his neck, draped there as a reminder of the curse that brought about the torturous destruction of the ship and the crew. Eventually, he was the only survivor and by then he was so wild-eyed just looking at him could drive you crazy.

After many trials, the ancient mariner prayerfully blessed a water snake that was swirling through a scummy sea and freed himself from his lousy bird.

The selfsame moment I could pray;
And from my neck so free
The Albatross fell off, and sank
Like lead into the sea.

Well, my "albatross" is still wrapped around my throat—it has been rotting there for some time now. And, by its very nature, my curse precludes absolution by prayer.

It's very late on this Saturday morning and I'll have to hurry. That's the best way to tell it anyway. Just the main details with an occasional digression to give it the right perspective.

I don't want to lose you, Newfriend. I need you.

You'll just have to believe me when I say I'm not some religious fanatic who has captured you for the purpose of offering salvation, or a criminal after your money, or some deviant who lusts for your body.

I'm not going to hurt you. And beyond any rational arguments I could use to command your attention, I've got the "glittering eye" today—you can't leave until I'm finished anyway. You might as well trust me.

It's Saturday morning and I need to tell someone what has happened. She always said I didn't talk enough—Maureen, that is. Maureen is, well actually, was my wife. You'd like her. She's very pretty but she doesn't live here anymore.

I'm going to talk now. Congratulations, you're going to hear the whole story, Newfriend. The entirety no one near or dear to yours truly has bothered to grasp.

I'll spare you lengthy description of all the plots and subplots and get to the heart of who I am, or what I am and a portion of the world I have known. If you go too far into anyone's life, it becomes very dull and I don't want you to be bored into not understanding. Telling more than the basic truths could endanger my purpose. You've had enough of the tediousness of soap opera in your own life, haven't you? The plots of my life, like yours, have, for the most part, been somewhat bland. They are created from such drudgery as divorce, injury, hidden loves, terror—the stock flow of experiences which already nearly distract you to death with your own life.

Please, just wait here with me for a while as I tell you what my wife, friends, and colleagues never began to understand. And I know what you are thinking. You're wondering why I'm foolish enough to believe a stranger will comprehend the needs and truths of my life that have eluded those who supposedly love me. That's the whole point of all of this. They—my wife, my friends, my colleagues–the people who love me, respect me, and, most of all, know me: I have never told them the story that has brought me to the solitude of this Saturday morning. It shouldn't have been necessary.

Are you ready now? Settled? Relatively comfortable? I won't ramble too much.

Deep in meditation one day about a year ago, a strange man walked into my brain and said, "This won't hurt."

He was a small and his face was almost completely hidden by a white monk's cowl. What little I did see of his face was white, like the face of a mime.

He pulled back the cloth slightly so as to reveal his smiling mouth as it repeated, "This won't hurt," and added, "don't worry."

Pulling a crossbow from beneath his robe, he handed it to me and said, "Shoot, please."

"Certainly," I said.

So, I shot an arrow, piercing a minute part of my brain. It didn't hurt. And, soft in the mantra rhythm of meditation I asked, "What have I done to my brain?"

"It is nothing," he said with the motion of an old smile. "You have merely severed a minor and useless sub-circuit in your communication network. You've eliminated a flaw, so to speak, and in doing so have cleared the way to experiencing higher consciousness."

"Thank you, thank you," I said with an amazing amount of sincerity and then, almost as an afterthought, I asked, "What is it I have cut out?"

"The bullshit," he said.

"Oh," I said.

PART ONE

Maureen

Chapter One
"...and I'm..."

It was not long ago, just a matter of about three weeks. I walked into this very apartment (it had furniture then) after enduring the challenge of an annual spring English teacher's convention for four days. Maureen met me at the door with an intense and serious face which I kissed.

I love her.

Then she started sobbing tears all down her cheeks— her nose running, wiping her nose with the back of her delicate hand, her voice breaking, her words muffled by the back of her hand and damp with sorrow. She said, over and over, "You're so good, you're so good...." Over and over.

I'm a very patient man. From years of experience, I knew my wife would always eventually reveal what was troubling her. But, regardless of any prompting on my part to expedite the telling of her truths, they were never spoken until she felt ready to speak.

So, while we are waiting for her, I'll tell you about the convention. It was terrible. The speakers were depressing. (They wanted machines to replace human beings, which has already happened anyway). The food was grease-on-a-bun purchased at fast food restaurants. (I couldn't afford the first-class fare at the "five-star" hotel where the convention was held.) The aristocratic environment of the place was offensive to my proletariat soul. (They still had housekeepers running around in little French maid costumes, and the male bellhops and porters wore drab purple tuxes the color of some moribund great aunt's parlor couch.) And I had fallen in love (with someone who, but for the most wistful of my recollections, might not even exist).

9

Louder sobs. Open crying.

I smiled sympathy at her and led her into the kitchen where I made myself a wonderful ham sandwich with cheese, pickle, and tomato on wheat toast. As I chewed, I thought how I wished I could help her.

I drank a glass of milk and found I was weary from the long drive across huge, snowy mountains and through twisting canyons. Maureen was still weeping and not yet ready to tell me anything of her sorrow.

I love her, you know.

I left her whimpering in the kitchen and went to the bedroom. I was too sleepy for my evening meditation so I undressed and climbed into bed.

Oh, it felt good to lie down on that good old bed and stretch out. As I left the kitchen, Maureen had added two words to her wet chant, making it: "You're so good, you're so good...and I'm...."

I rested my head on my favorite pillow (a thin feather pillow—I have always maintained that sleeping on thick pillows makes your chest sink in) when, gradually, I realized something was wrong. I sensed the presence of something alien to the eight-year, hallowed bed of our marriage. Something was amiss in our nest of bliss. Something was existent in our bed that was definitely extra-connubial.

What was it, you wonder? This might be a soap opera after all. Organ Music!

This damn bed smells like Melvin's aftershave, I thought.

"This damn bed smells like Melvin's aftershave!" I said, with considerably greater indignation than I had intended.

Maureen, bless her, came rushing into the room with a sob-soaked handkerchief covering most of her face. "Oh, Greg, Greg (that's my name, Newfriend, Greg Watkins. Glad to meet you), I didn't want to hurt you and now I have...." Her "have" bent into a whine and then more crying. A few throat-caught sobs and she finally blurted out, "You're so good. You're so good, and I'm going to leave you and marry Melvin."

Chapter Two
Hush

She stood there in the slant of light coming into the dark bedroom from the hallway. Upon her lovely face were tears and tear streaks. Her pretty eyes were squinted by the deep crease of her forehead. Her soft lips had become thin and inward in their tenseness.

"...Marry Melvin," she had said.

"Oh." I said, and for various reasons, both physical, and I'm sure, psychological, I went to sleep.

Isn't it funny, Newfriend, how the mind tries to protect us from levels of harshness we are unready to bear? It's like a dream of a school bell ringing. It's sounding the end of the day and you're a kid. It's ringing and ringing and you know it means you're about to be set free to rush through the school house door, hop on your bicycle, and ride the infinite reaches of the neighborhood world clear to dinner time. But, in fact, you're not a kid. You are a corporate drone or a rote-dull bureaucrat, the "school bell" is the old wind-up alarm clock your mother sent you off to college with, and it's clanging the hell out of the precious silence of dawn's early bedroom.

If the dream is persistent enough, the clock will eventually run down and slumber will have domain over obligation. But how rare it is indeed that we are blessed by such an obstinate dream.

Maureen was sobbing words I chose not to comprehend. So, I smiled at her, dropped lids, and drifted swiftly off into a deep sleep. And, just like with the imaginary school bell and the alarm clock, I sought flight in a dream.

It was a strange dream about being a miner, but I wasn't digging coal or gold. I was a lamp miner in the basement of a cavernous, old department store vibrating with the sounds of electric chimes and the voices of elevator operators saying things like, "Luggage, furniture, sporting goods, lamp shades...watch your step." I was deep into the dark, dark recesses of a lamp shaft when the shift boss started shouting, "Get up, you bastard! Get up!" And I tried to get up, but it was too late. There was a terrible cave-in and I was trapped while one particularly familiar pole lamp with red shades and bright gold chain hangers kept bashing me in the head.

"Get up, you bastard. Get up!" she said.

Before I go on with my story, I think I'd better tell you something about Hush Meditation. It's an important part of this. Hush Meditation saved my life, for all it's worth.

"Ninety-one dollars and fifty cents for peace of mind." That's what my friend, Jim, the insurance man, had said to me. I thought about it for a few days and asked him, "Then why is your stomach bleeding and why are you chewing your fingers?"

"What?" he asked defensively.

"Your life is just as screwed up as anybody else's."

"Well, I might have forgotten to meditate this year."

But what he said is true. I read about it in the highly respected journal, *The Scientific Citizen*. When they hooked up wires to people and told them to meditate, instruments indicated that good things happened to metabolism and heartbeat. The body was given profound rest, producing brain wave patterns deeper than those of lowest levels of sleep. Two short sessions a day and you're on the way to better times. And you could take the entire weekend course for the low, low price of $91.50.

It saved my life.

My friend Alice of the health food, Alice of the Earth, Alice of the Anti-Chemical Preservatives League, Alice of the "you are what you eat," best described my condition just prior to availing myself of the curative wonders of Hush Meditation. It happened a year and a half ago as we hiked over autumnal hills through high mountain aspen groves,

"Watkins, you might die right here because of all the grease and salt and chemicals and beer you've been dumping into your body. Watkins, you've got HBP, you hear, HBP!" I sat down on a rotting log and gripped my wrist, attempting to check my pulse. I imagined deep, throbbing, chest pains--perhaps a little dizziness, a pressure in my head.

"Dizziness? Pressure?" she asked with a wire-thin smile.

"Maybe," I said weakly.

"Watkins, with your HBP you'll have a stroke and be paralyzed and vegetate until you're lucky enough to have a heart attack and die."

Laboriously, I elevated my gaze from the ground and met her dancing eyes, "Thank you for your positive prognostication, Alice," I said darkly and cast my eyes back down to the earth. I could feel the stiffness setting in, no doubt, from my arteries turning to stone. My arms, dangled from slumping shoulders, ape-like, nearly brushing the dirt.

Then I realized that "HBP" was "high blood pressure." No wonder Alice was attacking me with such glee--she had it, too. (She always had that ruddy blush of arterial anguish about her.) I looked up and with eyes meeting hers and blending into a bond of mutual hostility, said, "You're glad I'm dying, aren't you?" She just laughed that female-liberation laugh of hers and jogged on over the hill to catch up with her boyfriend, Melvin, and my wife, Maureen.

It was right then, on an October afternoon a year and a half ago, sitting upon the rough bark of a fallen tree, that I accepted the fact that the course of my life was suicidal. I had known about my high blood pressure for over a year at the time. For a while I had taken little white pills every night until they quit being effective. The doctor (wizard in white) had prescribed new pills, which I took for about a week, and then Maureen and I had noticed they were making me impotent. This is to say, my old, faithful companion in delight would suddenly become extremely ineffective at the most critical of times. We weren't accustomed to such disappointment.

"Suicide," I said out loud as I kicked at the rubble of autumnal debris covering the forest floor at my feet. "If that's what this means, then that's what it is." Regardless of the dire consequences foretold by Alice, I was determined never to take another debilitating HBP pill in the, thank you, Alice, limited time remaining to my short life. I would willingly die a fully functioning man, rather than live long and limp as a medicated old codger.

Fortunately, at that time in my life there was another, less dire option available.

There was Hush Meditation.

"Why not?" I said. "Hell, I might even live."

Thus it was that Hush Meditation came to save my life.

It was the following Saturday when I started meditating under the tranquil guidance of my lovely little Guru-lady who said soft words like, "It is good. Yes?"

I would just nod from deep within the newly discovered, deep calm of my consciousness.

Two weeks without missing a morning or an evening meditation and I was changed.

At first, Maureen loved it. "Don't forget to meditate," she would say as she turned down the television.

The doctor loved it. "Your blood pressure is normal," he said.

And, most of all, I loved it. "I can be hard and hearty at the same time," I said.

But, you know, when I think about it now, Newfriend, "saved" is not really the right word to describe the effect meditation has had upon my life. A better word would probably be "prolonged." To "save" implies a kind of renewal, a salvation. To put it more accurately, meditation did not save my life, it extended it. There's a difference.

And you must be wondering what it was about my life that brought about the hypertension in the first place. The "grease and salt and chemicals and beer" of Alice's analysis were only irritants to a pre-existent tendency. You see, long before the physical effects of medicine and for reasons that to this very day I have yet to grasp fully, our bed was growing cold. I knew it. Maureen knew it. And, eventually, my body knew it.

Hush Meditation was a conscious means of protecting myself from an unbearable truth: my marriage was dying. Meditation was the obstinate dream.

And, speaking of dreams, when I awoke from my strange dream in the lamp mine, I found myself flat out in a bed in the Broken Head Ward of St. Ferd's Community Hospital.

Chapter Three
Herbert and other Hospital Horrors

Imagine this, Newfriend: A dimly lit room at St. Ferd's Hospital, the sound of rubber feet going busy-up and busy-down the hall. The antiseptic smell of steel-cold cleanliness.

That's where I awoke the morning after returning from the English teachers' convention, the morning after the night of Maureen's damp disclosure.

I'll tell you about it. I tumbled out of the nauseating void of semi consciousness to focus blearily upon the form of a lady in a business suit standing at the end of a hospital bed. She was motioning at me and to the person at her side. She was sternly staring at me as she spoke.

"My God!" I said. "My ass is hanging out!"

The ancient Egyptians' concept of hell was a dark and chilly place where thinly robed sinners milled around forever and never got warm. In addition to pyramids, I think they came up with the hospital gown.

"What happened?" I cried out from a dimming land of rolling dreams and swimming emptiness.

"Sir," said the business office lady with a severity to her voice that made me shiver even more, "I realize you have injured your head, but there is absolutely no excuse for obnoxious behavior and language. Now, demonstrate an iota of decency and kindly cover your bottom."

"So," I said as I quickly shifted the sheet, "it turns out that I'm a patient, after all."

I had realized I was in a hospital room for hours, but, until this woman started gesturing and shouting at me, I was reasonably certain I was a bedpan. I know it sounds weird, but I honestly had believed I was a big, white, metal "receptacle for the excreta of the bedridden" (Webster). Perhaps it was because of the metallic taste in my

16

mouth—concussions can give you that, you know. Yes, a bedpan, and I recall being horrified that someone was going to use me.

"We found him lying out in front of the hospital, bleeding on the sidewalk," she was saying to an orderly. The two of them shook their heads in disgust. "All he was wearing was a blood-stained tee shirt and undershorts. He didn't even have socks on his feet."

I shook my head, too. I felt so ashamed. "No socks?" I said in disbelief.

Ignoring me, she continued, "I really don't know where these kinds of people come from. I suppose he probably fell out of a boxcar as it rolled through town."

"Excuse me," I said cautiously for the sound of my own voice vibrated through my skull with excruciating pain. "Could you tell me...?"

"I'll tell you, all right, Sir. Do you think those bandages on your head are inexpensive? Do you think the fine resources of this medical facility are inexpensive? Do you think that the bed space you are filling is inexpensive?"

"No, ma'am, I'm sure it all costs a lot of money. But..."

"No 'buts' about it. It cost a great deal of money to care for the likes of you."

"But, I..."

Quiet!" she whispered crisply as she suddenly turned toward the door. She listened for a moment and then, with a soft, glowing smile turned to announce, "Hush, hush, everyone. It's the choir."

Granted, I was still hazy then and in an insubstantial region of verging consciousness, but I swear I think at least twenty women in white filed into the room, first humming and then, upon the execution of some subtle cue, singing in perfect unison. They were all there: the great, round, hairy nurses with enema bags slung from their shoulders like wineskins—singing bass; the sweet-mouthed young nurses with their uniforms opened one tantalizing button lower—singing sensual, breathy alto; the lab technicians with their vampire daggers clanging metallically at their sides like fencing foils—singing operatic soprano; and the dietitians with their aprons gray and splattered with nondescript patterns of colorless broth—humming a bagpipe-like drone behind it all. "There's the lady with the mop," I said, as she swished rhythmical splashes about the bed legs. And with multi-leveled harmony they sang to the tune of "Love Me Tender":

To the urine samples spilled
all down our hands and fingers,
to the vomit and the blood
and to the life that lingers;

Cheerfully, cheerfully, we offer up ourselves—
so you may end up healed and home,
or frozen on our shelves.

"What can I say?" I mumbled to myself as they filed back out into the gleaming hallway.

The admissions clerk and her clipboard were about to follow the choral ensemble on down the hall when I spoke up. "Could you call a nurse for me? I might be getting sick."

She spun about and barked, "Quit your complaining, there are deserving people who need care."

"But I..."

"But, what?" she demanded.

"But I've got insurance," I said.

Her mouth gaped into an oval and then recoiled into a great warm smile. "I hope we can be of good service to you, sir. Your health is our utmost concern." And then, rushing out the door she shouted down the hall, "Nurse, this man needs attention immediately."

See what a world we live in, Newfriend? What is the measure of our worth: our humanity or our Blue Cross?

Well, anyway, that wasn't the worst of my trials that difficult morning.

I'm still not certain about the dream-verses-reality status of the singing nurses, but what happened next in the saga of my stay at St. Ferd's was of such grating clarity that I could only wish it had been but a nightmare.

I received a visit from my brother-in-law.

I had been sleeping for a while. The fine folks of the St. Ferd's medical staff, upon notification of my fiscal accountability, had kindly provided me with a mild sedative. A couple of nifty pills and I just drifted away into the blessed respite of a silenced mind.

Then there came a terrible tapping upon my forehead.

Boy, did that hurt.

And again: Tap!

"This must be a dream," my mind cried. "Please, bring back the singing nurses."

"Wake up, sum-bitch, or next time I'll be a-hammerin' you with my handy ball-peen."

Night had been twisted with pain and semi-conscious sickness and now it was morning and Herbert.

Maureen's brother is a real character—a serious throwback to early forms of upright walking beasts genetically discarded by the process of evolution. It was eerie waking up with my headache subsiding just enough that I could, with great concentration, crack my eyes open without vomiting. And then there he was—splitting my cranium with his dirt-caked knuckles—Herbert, the brother-in-law.

Don't get me wrong. It isn't as if I didn't try to like the guy—you know, for the sake of the marriage. For years he and I used to drink beer together and burp and tell dirty stories out of our increasingly fictionalized pasts. We actually got along fairly well until one night last fall when I beat him at arm wrestling.

I've got to tell you about this, Newfriend. It's great. I worked on it for months—my funny little surprise for Maureen's ape-bodied brother. I bought a Sears Roebuck, five-spring, dynamic-tension chest expander. When I first brought it home, I ripped it out of the carton and attempted to pull it with all five gleaming steel springs attached. It was like trying to stretch a solid oak plank. I cut back to two springs, then, over a period of weeks, worked up to

19

three, and, finally, four (in the meantime, I had lost the fifth spring). Standing up with one handle hooked around a foot, I would vigorously stretch the other handle upward, one arm then the other. While sitting in the living room watching TV, I would precariously grip one end of the exerciser with my toes and repeatedly stretch the thing until my arms ached. Maureen would smile her soft and understanding smile at me as I sweated and panted through the evening news and on through late night reruns. She would say things like, "You asshole."

This was the grandest project of my life and, as I said, it worked. The culmination of my fiendish efforts occurred the evening before last Halloween. Herbert had come over to the apartment to tell me all the neat-o vandalism he had planned for the next night. He took particular pleasure in describing his intent to tap out the word "drat" upon the hood of his old high school English teacher's car—using his handy ball-peen hammer, of course.

"But, Herbert," I protested in mock alarm, "you're twenty-seven years old. You can't be going out acting like some malicious adolescent. Besides," I said with craft and premeditation, "what's the matter with English teachers anyway?"

"English teachers!" erupted Herbert in a froth of ghoulish laughter, "Fuckin'-A."

"Herbert," I chided. "Such language. Have you been hanging out with those coaches again?"

"Hey, you listen here, fella. You damn college boys and all your big words, what the hell do you draft-dodgin', milk-muscles ever do fur your flag-n-country? You bunch of prissy-assed bookworms never..."

"Hold on there, brother-in-law. Did I hear you say 'milk-muscled?'"

"Yeah," said Herbert, taking my artful taunt. "That's what I said. What of it, Mr. Ed-u-ca-tor?" The gleam of the easy kill glowed in his narrow eyes.

The table was quickly cleared, our fists locked, our eyes set.

Maureen walked through the kitchen and, glancing at us with an expression best described as null, said, "You assholes."

"Anytime, ditch-digger," I said in an even and dangerous tone. "This English teacher is ready!"

"Hell, Greg, ain't you started yet?"

Isn't that a wonderful story, Newfriend? Such a fine illustration of how goal-setting, dedication, and hard work can amount to success.

But what success in life is not eventually offset by the irony of fate? Looking up from the compromising perspective of a hospital bed, I shuddered at the realization that in my present condition he could beat me at arm wrestling or anything else.

He was talking to me and what could I do but listen? As a life-long student of the English language, Herbert's dialect has always amazed me. Maureen was reared in the same household and speaks perfect English—so do her parents. It is almost as if, in the formative years of his infancy, Herbert might have been locked away in a back room where a radio played country music twenty-four hours a day. "Jus think-a the good years that woman give to you and now look-it what you went and made her do," he was saying.

"Herbert," I said. "The size of your arms...I'll bet you've been working out at the gym again, haven't you?"

"Watkins, you'd better shut up and jus be a-listenin' to me now. You a-hearin' me, boy? I know you done cracked your stupid head, but I'm gonna crack it some more if I haf ta."

"You know, Herbert, sometimes I think you might be right. I might be a no good bastard after all."

"Now you're talkin' sense, brother-in-law. Damn right you're a no good bastard."

"Say, Herbert."

"Huh?"

"Just what the hell happened to me? Tell me, how did I crack my head? All I remember is going to bed last night with Maureen standing there telling me about Melvin, and the next thing I knew for sure was that I was in a hospital bed being scorned by some lady with a clipboard and an attitude. What happened, Herbert? I still don't know what's going on here."

Herbert looked at me with those muscle-eyes of his and shook his head. "You poor sum-bitch, you don't know, do you? Maureen tol' me the whole story on the phone las' night—tol' me all about it. How you started out meditatin' to save you lardy ass from high blood pressure and how it messed you up bad. She tol' me 'bout how she'd ask you normal stuff like 'Will you take out the garbage?' and 'Have you finished the income tax?' and 'Do you love me?' and how you quit even answerin' and would jus stare at her with the same silly grin on your ugly face that you're a-givin' me right now. It was plain to poor Maureen that you didn't give a damn about her. You ain't been washin' the car, policin' the lawn, combin' your damn hair, or nothin'. You quit doin' all the stuff that makes life more-n-a goldanged junkyard. You know, when she married you, we all said you was too weirdo for her, but we didn't think you'd turn into a cruel and heartless sum-bitch too."

I was getting tired of looking at Herbert and his bowl-trimmed, greasy hair draped in thick, dripping curls over his forehead. I was tired of listening to his story—I'd heard it from Maureen a thousand times anyway. So, I started meditating. Mantra, mantra, mantra, I thought. Mantra, mantra, policing the yard—hell, we don't even have a yard—mantra....

TAP!

It really hurt.

I probably felt a stronger sensation of physical pain at that moment than I had ever known in my life. Yes, good, old, Herbert, product of the same loins that had created my beloved Maureen, with a staccato tap of his trusty ball-peen hammer had given me new dimensions in pain.

I'll tell you about pain. I know I promised I wouldn't waste any time, Newfriend, but I'm going to tell you about Eddie Garkle and sixth-grade camp no matter if it does lose us a few minutes. Believe me, sometimes the worst things have got to be postponed. For years now, I've found that when it is difficult to handle a situation the best thing to do is justify some kind of diversion—sometimes there is sense in avoidance. Maybe you're strong enough to confront everything head-on. Good for you. I'm certainly not.

So, hang on a bit and I'll tell you about Eddie Garkle. It's not that long of a story.

Okay?

Eddie never could stand me. I haven't ever figured out exactly what terrible thing I did to make him hate me so much. He was one of those irate characters who hover about the edges of our lives and blame us for every misfortune that befalls his own petty existence. You know the type—you've likely met one or two of them in your life.

It was the third night of sixth-grade camp, late in the spring of my eleventh year. After a day of scaling fire towers, carving scary faces in sandstone bluffs, shooting arrows with fifteen pound bows, eating vast, meat-and-vegetables-clockwise, milk-pitcher-counterclockwise dinners, and spending a laugh-filled evening around the camp piano singing "The Bear Went Over the Mountain" I retired to my little cot in the back corner of "Cabin Six" and quickly succumbed to a very deep sleep.

Through bad luck of the draw or perhaps the pernicious cruelty of the Fates, Eddie Garkle had been assigned to my cabin. Throughout the first three blissful days of camp week, he and I had been programmed into the same sequence of character- and body-building activities. He'd had a miserable week. I later found out his mother was coming to pick him up the next day because he had developed a rash. I think he knew that night was to be his last chance to get me before repairing to the distant dermatologist in the morning. He had already succeeded in hitting me with a cow-pie at the dairy farm demonstration and spitting on my head as we climbed up the fire tower but, it seemed, his need for inflicting misery upon me had not been sufficiently satisfied. To this day, I believe, for some, rage is an unquenchable force with which to reckon.

That night, after I had wearily drifted off to dreams of green mountain forests and giggling girls in the camp shower, he administered a torture of his own creation to my slumbering body producing an experience in pain that held the record for over twenty years. Hours into the black night, he crept to my bedside, pulled open the security of my little eyelid, and crammed one of those pea-sized, spiked burrs into my baby-blue left eye.

Boy, did that hurt—the revenge of Eddie Garkle's rash back there at sixth-grade camp. It hurt so badly that I had blanked most of what it felt like from memory until Herbert tapped my concussed head and then, in a moment, Eddie Garkle and legions of pain- and irritation-causing creatures conjured from my past were standing there with all of their distorted eyes on Herbert and their twisted mouths saying, "Wow, Herbert. Right-on, right-on. Allll right!"

"Don't you go a-pullin' any of that meditation crap on me, you bastard."

"Go to hell, Eddie Garkle," I said.

"Ja-ezz-us crimony gosh, you are nuts, Watkins," he said and then he moved close to my face like the country music singers he so dearly loves get when they sing harmony into a single microphone. I could smell his air.

"Drove that good woman off with your give-a-shit attitude, drove her out of the sanctity of marriage to the arms of a man who truly cares, drove her to leave you las' night when you finally flipped out an' hit yourself in the head with a lamp, drove her to leave you las' night an' move to Myrtle Beach with Melvin. Drove her..."

"'Hit myself in the head,'" I said. "They really believe that?"

"Uh...yeah. Yeah, sure. And not only all that, but poor Maureen was so torn-up about your...uh...accident she couldn't even bear to stay around to see if you lived. She told me to stay here 'til you was one way or t'other an' I says to her 'hell yeah' I'd hang around. She said she didn't think she could face you and have you jus' go to sleep again anyway, or somethin' like that—now, what the hell are you laughin' about, Greg? There ain't nothin' funny

24

about this here situation. This here is serious business. How the hell can you be layin' there laughing when you've got a busted head and your old lady's left town?"

I laughed really hard. My wife could have killed me. The love of my life had clubbed me half to death with our pole lamp, Newfriend. My wife. It's not easy to deal with now, weeks later just sitting here telling you about it. I hate this. Imagine what I felt like then—flat out on a hospital bed with Herbert being the bearer of the terrible news.

It was an awful thing to accept—so I laughed. Maybe I was hoping Herbert would whack me another peen-tap. It would have hurt less.

So I laughed. It felt good to have tears in my eyes. I laughed and laughed—Herbert could have never understood that I was laughing a mad version of Abbott and Costello's "Who's on First?"

Who's in love? Who's in Myrtle Beach? Who's in the hospital with a broken head?

"Well, one thing, good buddy..." I laughed.

"Yeah?"

"I say, Herbert, it could be worse."

He just looked at me blankly.

"I could be a bedpan."

Chapter Four
"Greg, you're no good."

As I tell you these details of my life, I have to face them myself. Sometimes it's not easy.

It is difficult to talk about my wife beating me in the head with a pole lamp. It's not easy to face the fact that my actions generated such rage in someone whom I love and who loves me. But they did. I've got the wounds to prove it.

And speaking of life's little agonies, I believe this will be a good time to tell you about Melvin. Every time I start thinking I'm lower than the nurf-fuzz in a serpent's belly-button, I think about Melvin and, what the heck, maybe I'm not so bad as I thought. Yes, Newfriend, I'll tell you about Melvin. Just thinking about that low-life scum makes me feel better already.

Melvin.

Melvin who stole my Maureen away from me and carried her far off to the Eastern Sea.

Melvin is my friend. I love him. My mother said he would always be my friend and that I should love him because he was my brother.

So I did.

You've got to understand who Melvin is if you're going to understand any of this. In some form or another, throughout my life I have been playing "straight man" for Melvin in his fantastically successful, starring role in the comedy of our lives.

Don't get me wrong. I'm not bitter. I don't hate Melvin Watkins. I don't envy my brother and his financial empire, his beach homes on both coasts, his private jet. I love my brother.

I have to admit, though, there have been instances over these recent weeks, sitting alone in this void of an apartment, when it has been difficult to heed the desire of my mother regarding my dear brother. Moments sitting here just as you are now, next to the window that overlooks the front sidewalk (except that until quite recently I enjoyed the luxury of chair ownership and didn't have to sit on the rug). Moments, hell, hours spent staring down at that damned empty sidewalk waiting for Maureen to come back and knowing that for all my wishing and waiting she never will.

No, I don't resent Melvin. But sometimes the thought of that beady-eyed, money-grubbing, son of a bitch (no offence, Mom, just a figure of speech) nuzzling his smug-ugly face between the warmth and wonder and magnificence of Maureen's great, big, naked tits is enough to drive me crazy. I swear it makes me want to scream!

Ahhhhhhhhhhhhhhhhhhhhhhhhhhhhh!

Sorry, Newfriend. I didn't mean to get so emotional. Sit back down. There's nothing to worry about. It won't happen again, I promise...maybe.

I'll tell you about Melvin and then maybe we'll both have a good scream. I've got so much I could tell you—so many episodes in the saga of an asshole. Let me see....

One day when we were walking home from school—I think I was about nine, Melvin would have been ten—Melvin grabbed my jacket sleeve and pulled me aside from the other kids. He told me, as a trick we'd play on the gang, we would act like we were fighting and I was to throw him down a hill. He would roll out into the street and all the kids who were watching would say, "Look at that Greg. He sure is strong."

"Do you really think so, Melvin?" I asked with a cautious skepticism borne of many dupings.

"Yeah. I'm sure."

"Now what am I supposed to do?"

"Just throw me down the hill, stupid. We'll pretend we get into an argument and then, when everyone is watching and wondering what's going to happen next, we start shoving each other. Right? Then you push me and I'll roll

27

all the way down the hill and into the street and everyone will say, 'Wow, look at that Greg. I sure wouldn't want to mess with that Greg. He sure is a strong one.'"

I said, "Very well, Melvin. I will throw you down the hill, but be real careful, for there are many cement trucks that travel this highway."

He said, "Don't worry, Gregory, it will all be fun and you will look so good in front of the whole gang."

We rejoined the straggling line of homebound children on the path and I thought about his plan. "Say, Melvin, why are you doing this for me? Why are you going to go to such trouble to make me look good? You don't even like me very much."

"This is true," he said, "but, I do sometimes feel bad for always making a fool of you in front of the gang. This will make us both feel better."

"Gee, Melvin," I said.

It wasn't really a big hill—actually; the path was just cut into the side of a steep grass terrace, perhaps twenty-five or thirty feet up from the road.

There was a bunch of us kids walking along the path that day. School had just been let out and every day we all would rush to get off the playground and start the walk home where we could say mean things like "Sandra Hardy has Texas cooties" and "Eat it raw, Chester."

Many, many energetic faces and one lovely, lovely face. Lou Anna Martin.

Oh, how I loved Lou Anna Martin. I was only nine but I knew she made me feel good and miserable at the same time. And every day I demonstrated my love for her. She seldom brought paper and pencils to school, so, I gave her mine and would borrow from her. I gave her my whole academic kit: A "Big Chief" tablet of lined paper and the pencil box my mother had so lovingly assembled for me. But, for some reason Lou Anna never rose to my defense when the teacher would scream, "Gregory, where is your paper? Where are your pencils, your eraser, your ruler, your scratch pad? Why don't you ever show up for class properly prepared like Lou Anna? You mustn't depend on the generosity of others to get you by."

But I didn't care. I just thought of her sweetly as I wrote three-hundred-sixty-five times: I will remember to bring my materials to class every day of the year.

I didn't care. I was in love.

And I was convinced that, in her own way, Lou Anna kind of cared for me too. I believed it because sometimes she would tickle me as I hung from the 10-foot-high pipe across the top of the monkey bars. I would giggle all the way down to the pavement below. As I would lie there in a disjointed splat, I would listen to the titter and lilt of her laughter singing from far above. I can hear it right now, Newfriend.

How I loved that little girl.

I knew Lou Anna Martin would be watching so I was willing to commit the mock humiliation of my beloved brother. And, as we started yelling, "You did!" "I did not!" "Liar, liar, house on fire!" I was thinking, "Gee, what a neat-o brother I have to let me look good in front of Lou Anna Martin. How very selfless of him, for I know that he, too, loved my dear Lou Anna for he mentioned her precious name in his sleep."

"Now," he whispered.

"Huh?" I replied.

"Now!"

"Oh, yeah," I said as I greedily glanced back to see Lou Anna watching intensely with her pretty, rose-red lips parted in that devilish smile of hers.

I shoved, and, with grace and terrible momentum, Melvin tumbled down the spring-soft grass toward the deadly street.

That Melvin was such a good actor. With "oomphs" and "awks", he dramatically punctuated his decent down and down the hillside. Everyone was watching while he rolled and rolled and rolled right under a cement truck and was killed.

"Oh, no..." said the gang. And while we waited for an ambulance to come and cart away his road-flat remains, six of my best friends hit me with rocks and Lou Anna sat at his fat, little side looking up at me and crying, "Greg, you're no good."

The rescue squad never did arrive because the cement truck turned out to be Melvin's gigantic, cardboard, chicken wire, and four-bicycle idea of a joke.

Boy, did the gang laugh at that. Especially Lou Anna Martin.

When we got home and my mother asked me what had happened to my face and why did I look like I had been stoned, I said, "Don't worry, Mom. It's all right. I just fell face first into a gravel pit."

Funny guy, that Melvin. And quite the competitor, too. For example, Melvin is a year and a couple of months older than I am and has such a compulsive sense of competitiveness that he actually feels he achieved a real victory over me by being born first.

I really can't tell you the source of Melvin's nature. It's almost like my brother-in-law Herbert's bumpkin drawl—a behavioral aberration not a product of either of his parents. Our father was never what one would call a "go-getter." He taught me to live with the flow of life. When every family in the neighborhood bought a parakeet back in '54, the year of the parakeet rage, my father, on one of his strolls through the dump, found a discarded birdcage. He proudly returned home with his prize and announced that we, too, could have a parakeet. Melvin was ecstatic. He said, "Make it a big one, Dad, biggest in the neighborhood and I'll make it talk."

I even got excited. "When can we go buy one, Dad? Today? Huh? Today?"

I got my answer a few moments later. You see, after fate had given us a perfectly good (with a little baling wire and sheet metal) birdcage, my father sat down in back of the house with a cup of coffee and the Sunday Post and waited.

Time passed. Everyone had televisions and extension phones were no rarity. Cars with huge rear fins and gaudy chrome grills were in, as were Cocker spaniels and "Let's

Go to the Hop," when, on a late summer's evening in 1958, Dad gleefully ran into the house with the blood-and-feather wreck of a tiny green bird that had crash-landed in the backyard. "Here's the parakeet!" he shouted. "Somebody get the cage!"

So you see, the kind of drive that was manifest in Melvin's meteoric grovel to the top of the financial and upper class social communities, and which is yet, obviously, alive and well in the execution of his personal life, wasn't chipped off of our father's "old block." Nor was my mother the source of such an amoral appetite for obnoxious accomplishment.

One New Year's Eve when I was about eleven, the Sweeneys came over to our house for a party. Some other people were there, several families in fact, and, purely as a matter of coincidence—for no one would contrive such a thing—everyone brought pickled herring.

It was Mr. Sweeny who started it by saying, "Boy, do I love these salty, little fishies." And then in the slurring tones of a drunken challenge, he added, "An' I can eat more pickled herring than anybody I know."

My father said, "It's a real pleasure to know you, Champ."

And my mother just said to Mr. Sweeny, "Sounds sickening to me, Sherman."

And Melvin, who was way down the hall hogging all the popcorn from the other kids and me by eating with both hands and with most of his head burrowed deep into the pan, cried out, "My dad can eat more pickled herring than anybody!" and took off at a run for the kitchen.

All of the other kids followed. One of them grabbed the pan of popcorn so I followed, too. I arrived in the kitchen just in time to hear Dad mutter, "Say, Melvin, why don't you shut up about the damned fish."

But it was too late. The party had centered around Dad and Mr. Sweeney and there was no escaping the contest. I saw the hopeless look on Dad's face and the slightly green tint to Mom's. I saw the excitement beaming out of Melvin's eyes. "Come on, Dad, you can show him," he said.

A half-hour later, Mrs. Sweeney said, "Sherman, I think you are going to pass out from all the whiskey you've been drinking to wash down those awful slimy fish. Now why don't you men call this silly contest a draw and quit eating that garbage?"

"Yes! Yes, why don't we do that? You know, just call it even and quit," Dad said. "Why, you might even be a couple ahead of me—as a matter of fact, I'm sure you are. Yes, you win, you win. I quit, you win, it's over."

But then, from his vantage point on top of the kitchen counter, Melvin, with handy, pocket ledger and needle-sharp, #2 pencil in hand, said, "I believe you're mistaken, Father. My calculations show that there is an exact tie at this moment. Right kids?" And, as usual, they had all joined Melvin, including the kid with the popcorn, and eagerly concurred with grins and rapid head-nods.

"Jes one little ole fishy an' I'll win," slobbered Mr. Sweeny as he flopped his face flatly upon the table and passed out.

Dad got up to help Mrs. Sweeny gather the limp remains of her husband when Melvin grabbed his arm and said, "You've got him now, Pop. Just eat one more and you win."

Mom rose abruptly from the kitchen table where the adults had been gathered and announced, "Well, Daddy, if you eat one more of those nasty fish you're going to get sick, and I'm not going to wait around here and watch." With that, she turned and left the room.

Dad, who was a bit miffed at Mom's dire prophecy and abrupt exit, looked about the room for approval and said, "Hey, one more won't really matter, will it?"

Melvin said, "Ya gotta, Dad. Ya Gotta."

And all his coterie of kids chanted, "Eat one more! Eat one more! Eat one more!"

And all the adults (except Mr. Sweeny, of course) just smiled with their teeth (even Mrs. Sweeny).

So, with a somewhat sheepish smile of confidence, Dad gulped down the deciding herring, suddenly paled, and rapidly stepped out on the back porch and threw-up.

Melvin started the noisemakers up and the firecrackers and ran in and out of the house shouting, "We won! We won! I won!"

After the din had settled, Melvin, with his voice echoing from deep into the final inches of the popcorn pan, had retired to a distant corner of the house and, to the youthful legion of admirers, was retelling his heroic role in the epic battle of the pickled herring, and Mrs. Sweeny was wandering about mumbling, "Where'd the damn fool leave his hat?" when, from the solitude of the living room, in a voice spoken to the shadowy form just out the back door, my mother said, "Well, Daddy, how's it feel to be a winner?"

Melvin Watkins is a genetic enigma. I might be poor, I might be ugly, I might not be real bright but, by damn, I'm not an asshole. My parents aren't assholes. But, sure as hell, my brother is an asshole.

One more story. I promise I'll stop then. Jesus, I could go on for hours. But, just one more.

I was fifteen; he was sixteen and neither of us had gotten any. It was a source of discomfort and need for me, but for Melvin it was a horrific disgrace that he had already lost the race to several of his buddies. His only salvation lay in the fact that I, too, was a virgin and might yet be defeated.

And, to hear him tell it, what a race it was. Of course, he won.

It happened up the street from our house where the Rigby sisters seemed to always babysit. It was an absolute truth in town that the Rigbies would ball anyone for a six-pack of Pabst Blue Ribbon beer. Having tried all the normal channels of amorous pursuit with the less infamous females in our realm with no success, and having found a procurer of illicit spirits down at the local 7-11, we proceeded to the site of the proposed Rigby seduction.

"You talk to them, Greg."

Knock. Knock.

Pause.

"Maybe they're not here tonight. We'd better go," I said with an obvious sense of relief.

"Damn it, Greg, they're here. I know they are—I have my sources. Knock again."

Knock! Knock!

I nearly jumped off the porch when the door swung open and one of the girls said, "Yeah? What do you guys want?"

"Um...err...."

"Tell them, Greg."

"Err...uh, Ginger and Kelly, err...we'd like..."

"Got any Pabst Blue Ribbon?" she demanded.

"My God, it's true," I whispered to Melvin.

We showed them Six-Pack #1.

Kelly Rigby, the harder of the two thick-fleshed girls, said, "Let's see your rubbers."

We dug for our wallets with clumsy hands and with near-useless fingers delved deep into hidden places (normally easily discerned, for our wallets were permanently embossed with their imprint) and extracted our dubious security.

"They look kind of old," said Ginger while plying one with her fingers.

Kelly opened the package, unrolled mine a few turns and blew into it like a balloon. Holding it up to the porch light, she said, "Well..."

With a conspiratorial glance and the rustle of a grocery sack, Melvin and I proudly produced Six-Pack #2.

Twin beds.

Twin beds and in the shadowy room clothing had been tossed about and everyone was naked.

And I thought: She's really naked. Ginger Rigby and Greg Watkins, two naked people. Me naked, her naked, us naked....

"Hey, are you going to do this or what?"

And my mind mused on...she didn't look nearly so fat when she had her clothes off. God, real tits, real pubes. "I might be in love," I said.

"Are we going to screw, or are we going to just stare at each other all night?"

"Okay. Sure, I'm going to do it. Now...err...where?"

"Are you kidding me?"

"Well, I know it's down there somewhere, but, I've never..."

In the dim light I could see a grin, no, a smile of simultaneous forgiveness and disbelief that yet lingers in my memory, as Ginger guided me with her artful hands and I was inside of my first woman. Inside. Really inside.

Melvin was squeaking the other bed furiously while I rolled slowly in the soft, soft flesh of Ginger Rigby.

"Ahhhhhhhh! Wow! Ahhhhhhhhh," yelled Melvin. And then, "I won, I won. I beat you Greg. I went first. I beat you."

"Yes, you did," I said.

"Oh, yes, he did," said Ginger and it was all air-breathing sounds and exhilaration.

Later, as we lay in silence—me grinning and trying to keep from giggling because I felt so good, and her smoking a cigarette and, not to boast, apparently feeling pretty good herself—I heard them get up. I heard the sound of a beer can opening, then Kelly's first words since the throes of love, "Oh great, the beer's warm."

Had enough "Melvin Stories," Newfriend? I've got a million of them. Too bad there isn't time to tell them all, right?

No doubt about it, my brother is a genuine, red-blooded-American, class "A" prick. He's got big cars, big houses, and a massive ego to match, and now it turns out that the bastard is a big jerk, too.

And, get this, Newfriend, right at this very moment, he's probably wrapping his sticky self six times around my beautiful, sensitive, warm-breasted, bed-wonderful, eight-years-of-my-god-forsaken-life, breathing, tasting, moving woman.

Ahhhhhhhhhhhhh!

Would you care to join me?

AHHHHHHHHHHHHHHHHHHHHHHHHHHHHHHHHHHHHH HHHHHHH!

Chapter Five
Help!

You don't perceive your wife's sorrow and discontent in a five-minute sob-session. Awareness of the extent of your hopelessness and isolation as a human being doesn't strike like lightening at the whiff of extra-marital aftershave wafting up like some ghastly apparition from your bed pillow (the bastard). The process of alienation takes years to evolve and can be charted by symptomatic breakdowns of increasing severity at various stages. But sometimes it isn't until the final moments of absolute dissolution that the development becomes so patently clear. If you doubt what I'm telling you, just tune in any major network station five afternoons a week and watch the whole miserable process in living color. What I'm trying to say is, the death of a marriage might begin the night the wife quits walking her husband to the door when he takes out the trash, years before she starts having an occasional fling with the guy down the street. Or, long before hubby finds himself creeping in the back door, hoping she doesn't hug him and smell somebody else's perfume.

The night of the brain bashing was just the end of an extended sequence of losses—not the beginning.

I had been seeking love elsewhere before she committed the final and, probably, most honest act by running away with Melvin (the bastard). I've got to tell it all, regardless of what opinion you might form of me. To omit any part of this would be dishonest—it would be bullshit.

There was Millie, a loving physical outlet for the rage of my rejected manhood, but I'll tell you about her later. First, I'll tell you about Amy who just three short weeks ago filled my heart with love and it mate, emptiness.

I remember every detail.

"What are we supposed to be doing out here? I don't think I quite grasped it all," the girl had said with such a pretty smile.

"I'm not really sure. Maybe we should go back inside and ask the lady to give us her two-hour lecture one more time just to get it right."

And she laughed. Oh, the laugh that rose on butterfly wings from the heart of the girl with such a pretty smile.

"My name is Amy," she said, "and, if you don't mind, I'll pass on a rerun of Dr. Feller's rambling 'Mysteries of the Physical Sphere.'"

And I laughed and she liked the ease and honesty of my laugh so we walked together for a half an hour and fell in love. Or, at least I did.

"I'm Greg," I had said.

It was the boring conclusion of a boring day of workshops at the English Teacher's Convention. The professor had said:

Seek the non-verbal in the shapes of your world. Go out and find the functions of man—his art, his livelihood—in the mountain shadows and the mirror lake, in the spiraling towers, in the sculptured greenery of the golf course, in the subtle color of the brick. For half-an-hour, wander the magnificent grounds of this fine old hotel and gather.

"Gather," she had said.

Her final charge before freeing us from the bludgeon of her verbiage was, "Go now in pairs. Gather! And when we regroup on the terrace, we will share with one another the wonders of the non-verbal. The mysteries of the physical sphere."

And with a developed eye for such manipulation, I walked out the glass door with a lovely young lady.

Her name, you know, was Amy. I was reasonably certain immediately, and, after a few short minutes of "wandering" with her laughter and her eyes and the texture of her spirit, I was finally certain that I would love her all the remaining days of my existence.

Hold on a minute, Newfriend. I've got to interrupt this.

It's happening right now and I'll try to tell you what I mean. You see, this is a story of the isolation of a sensitive yet, at times and with specific reason, non-communicative human being: me. A man blessed with vision but cursed by honesty.

It's bad right now, I'll tell you, it's bad. This special awareness, this special need that has no voice. I'm trapped in this place where no one on Earth can help me, or even wants to help me. It's a lonely place where I am. And even you wouldn't be here if it were not for my mesmerizing glare. Admit it. You're stuck here with some raving maniac when you'd rather be down at the VFW doing a polka and pinning five-dollar bills on the bride's titties. Right? I don't blame you, but it is true, isn't it? But for the captive attention you're forced to give me, I am alone in this world.

Everyone has a "wedding party" somewhere, and we're all alone with our needs and our fears.

Do you know what love is, Newfriend? You think it's lust and companionship and sharing, don't you?

Not really.

How can we share what only we alone are allowed to understand, each of us isolated by our unique set of perceptions? It's true, love is lust: lust for help and touch and proof that we are real—validation of our souls that wander nearly lost in the myth of reality. "Love me!" we cry out. "Embrace me with the intimacy of your sex and your secrets; your mind and your tax-sheltered annuities. Hold me!" we implore. "Don't ever let me go. Gather the seeds of our pleasure in our collective womb and nurture eternity with me."

But, in truth, love is just two people holding hands in a movie theater and yet, no matter how tightly their fingers intertwine, how closely they lean the perimeters of their bodies, how intensely they perceive the scent, the warmth, the touch of each other's huddled existences, they are watching two entirely different movies.

I told you I would fill in a few details while we waited together. Okay, I'll do that and, believe me, there are more stories to tell and experiences to give: Facets of my odyssey that I am capable of verbalizing. But, for a moment, here, in the middle of beautiful Amy's story, let me tell you what this predicament of mine is all about.

The story is only the edge.

I'm trying to tell you about the hopelessness of contiguous, yet, non-communicative spheres of existence.

There. I've said it. I feel much better now.

Let me try again. It is the eight-layered existence of a being combined with that of other seven-, ten-, five-layered existences with no cross-over except on the most basic levels so we can tell one another, "The bathroom is down the hall, diner will be ready in ten minutes, wanna do it, Johnnie flunked, Grandma died, the refrigerator is hot." But, nothing about, "I'm so lonely. Please hear me."

Today I am so alone.

I've always been alone, but in the sun-brutal honesty of this Saturday morning all the marvelous distractions have been stripped away and I am so alone.

Love is the best of all distractions. And now, this curse of honesty has taken even that away. I could not honestly grovel in the small talk of petty affection when my feelings were so profound. When I communicated to Maureen, "I love you," in the subtlety and power, the silence of the spiritual, emotional, intellectual language of Level #8, she heard, "I don't care," in the pedestrian patter of Level #2.

That's why she left me.

I think.

You see, don't you, why the story must be so very long to tell a moment's feeling. Why it has to reach all around to touch my small message.

I am desperate, alone, disheartened, untouching, untouched. And the irony of my honesty is that, more than anything, I need help right now but I can only truthfully speak from the level of my need. It would be dishonest to say less.

But I'll try anyway. I'll try the same way I've been trying for months.

I'm going to try to ask for help. I believe Level #7 is honestly the closest I can come to normal expression of such a deep-felt need.

Listen. Please.

" _ _ _ _!"

See what I mean? Well, anyway, on with my story. At least there are words to describe actions even if there are none to tell needs.

Heart-deep love struck cynical ole Watkins on the sculptured shore of a hotel duck pond and, just like it hits the synthetic characters in supermarket romance novels, good ole, sophisticated, sarcastic Watkins stood there looking up at the adobe towers and said, "I like being with you, Amy."

And she said, "I like being with you, too."

So went thirty beautiful minutes. We didn't really say many words but we laughed and we looked at each other and listened to the silence that spoke so clearly. And then she said, "I've got to go, Greg. My fiance is picking me up in five minutes and I'd better be out front."

"Goodbye, Amy. I hate to lose you so soon."

"Goodbye, Greg," she said.

And she walked around the corner of the hotel and was gone forever.

And I said to the emptiness where she had been, "I love you."

I haven't told this well enough, have I, Newfriend? I mean, you're not feeling it like I want you to feel it. Granted, it's not the hottest love story you've ever heard but, at least it's true. You see, it was me, Greg Watkins, Maureen hadn't left yet, but she was about ready to, and I was wandering through an incredibly dull convention filled with sexless lady English teachers wearing sexless strong perfumes and carefully confusing hair. Me, bitter; me, only existing, and then in one short half hour what had been apathetic and hopeless became loving and empty and hopeless like never before.

41

I'll try to tell you why I love Amy. She was pretty and showed me she was listening and telling with her eyes and her aura when there was talking and, also, when no words were spoken. She had a laugh that spilled easily from her spirit to vibrate through my soul. She laughed at my jokes. She... well, it seems, Newfriend, I am no more capable of saying "love" than I am saying "help." It's all soaring in such celestial realms, to such heights that the clumsy symbols of a language anchored in the self-defensive mire of the mundane can't even approximate its wonder or its need.

But I did write down her address. The workshop session was reconvening on the terrace. The lady was beginning to flow again about the treasures of shape, form, time, and on and on. Beside her, on a chair, sat the list of workshop people and I leaned toward the lady as if listening more carefully and stole my Amy's address.

That night, in my cheap motel way down the road from the rich and pseudo-rich, I wrote her a note which I mailed the following day.

I only said:

Dear Amy,

Do you understand?

Love,
Greg

Chapter Six
Experiences While Meditating

Maureen eventually developed an intense hatred for my meditation. She said after the first couple of weeks it changed me from a nice guy into a real jerk. I would counter with a smile, "I haven't changed. It's just taken you all these years to realize whom you married."

I made light of her complaint, but, the fact is, meditation has changed me. I have learned of a whole world within my being which can't be spoken, only known. I'll tell you about the periphery of my experience, the only part that can be shared—the crust of being we call reality. You, Maureen, and the whole rest of the physical world are excluded from the interior. That's probably why Maureen thought meditation had made me cold and insular. By the very definition of "interior" she was left out.

To realize the full benefit of Hush Meditation, you have to meditate for fifteen minutes in the morning and again in the afternoon. Scheduling such seemingly nonproductive moments into a life cluttered with obligation can be difficult. We have to steal time from the demands of others. It's the only way.

You're not supposed to eat before you meditate because the food won't digest while you are humming through the cosmos and you get a bellyache. Also, if you drink beer before you meditate it interferes with the subtle consciousness and other things. So, what I did was meditate behind the bookshelves in a book storage closet at school in the morning, and then have my morning orange and, on special occasions, my morning beef jerky. In the afternoon I would usually cloister myself in an empty classroom and fall asleep. (Maureen used to joke about that. "Ha, ha," she would say. "Sure you were meditating. It's nine o'clock and you were just meditating." And I used to joke back, "No, Maureen, actually I was down at the Grover Apartments screwing Silly Little Millie.")

Meditation is very quiet. You only speak with your mind and you don't breathe very much. (Sometimes your stomach growls because you are usually starving due to the required, two-hour fast in avoidance of gas.) If people don't see you, you are invisible; and, to any more than memory or the happenstance of mention, to the outside world you don't exist. I'll tell you about some of the strange and wonderful and terrible experiences I have known while being invisible.

The book room was not always as silent as a good place of meditation should be because it was far from being a normal book storage closet. My friend, Wes the English teacher, and I and several other English teachers moved the ceiling-high book shelves closer together, donated lamps, added a throw rug, a couple of slightly worn easy chairs, a desk, a typewriter, and a coffee pot and called it the English Department Office. It became a haven from the gossip and sports talk that had previously been the substance of a conference period. Wes and I had our break time scheduled first period and on many mornings started our days sharing the quiet confines of an upstairs closet. People would stop in and say, "Hello, you lazy, soft-assed, antisocial English teachers." And we would say, "Get your eyes off the big soft chairs, O' envious ones."

Wes and I talked serious matters down, laughed about a world we could only bear with humor, bitched about policy, and mused about the pretty senior girls and their bosoms and butts. It wasn't a bad place, considering that it was located within the dreaded confines of an institution of learning.

I would sit in there before school on a wooden chair I placed as far back in the dark shelves as possible. My mind would say my mantra, the meditative phrase ceremoniously given to me by my Guru-lady, over and over and I would go deeper and deeper into a quiet rest within myself. My friend, Harvey the math teacher, would sit on the other side of the shelf in one of the big, soft, English Department chairs and mutter questions about inequitable treatment and incompetence. Sometimes I would answer; sometimes I would be too deeply involved to return to the shallow level of spoken words.

Once, while in the lunchroom, I heard a conversation between two of the dozen or so coaches who inhabited the school. One said, "Hey, Otto, I know that fuckin' Harvey was nuts but he's even worse than I thought. I swear to God he sits upstairs every morning in some goddamned closet talking to himself."

On to the experiences.

One morning when Harvey was gone (come to think of it, most of the experiences that are memorable occurred on days when Harvey was gone) and I was deeply immersed in the process of becoming spiritual essence, Miss Ark, the English teacher, peeped into the seemingly empty room. She was the most stereotypical old bag of a lady English teacher I had ever met. Her clothes were severe, her glare disapproving, her body rigid, her work perfect, and her students terrified. I would watch her at faculty coffees and I don't recall her ever dropping a cookie crumb on her perfect lap. Her life was order; her work, a masterpiece of propriety. And in a ridiculous, guilt-ridden way, she scared the hell out of me.

But, on the morning of the meditative encounter, her normal assurance was lacking. With furtive glances, she looked up and down the hallway and then around the book room, closed the door, walked to a back corner, and blew a giant, cheese-factory fart.

I told you there were wonderful times.

And terrible, too. Far, far within, without, and beyond the protection of my bookshelves I heard three people, the teachers, wander into the closet and start talking to Harvey. One finally said, "Hey, guess what, Harvey. Remember that Mexican kid, George Martinez?"

"I think I do," Harvey replied. "He had problems in my class. All he ever wanted to do was draw pictures in his notebook. He never seemed to pay attention."

"Yeah, he's the one—had long hair and a crooked nose, used to go with Peggy Thomas. God, did she have big tits. I never could understand what she saw in that little wetback."

"Peggy always passed my classes," interrupted a teacher.

"What about George?" asked Harvey.

"Oh, yeah. He drowned in the river last night. Probably drunk, he fell off the Fifth Street Bridge.

And then the teachers said, "What was that sound behind the shelf?"

"Oh no..." I had said. George Martinez. Once he told me that someday he would give those red-necked sons-of-bitches something to talk about.

And there were erotic, voyeuristic times, too.

One afternoon I altered my normal pattern of using an empty classroom and started meditating in the book room, which, for some reason, was almost empty.

The last teacher left and turned out the lights, but I didn't care. I had my eyes shut anyway. I didn't need to see my watch to judge fifteen minutes anymore.

Humming peace, escape—comfort filling my mind in the windowless dark. Deep quiet. When you're successfully meditating, sometimes the sound of a bug scratching his ear will split you in half.

Split! I jumped as the door swung open.

"See," said Mr. Vincent, the esteemed principal of the high school. "I told you those English teachers were having a meeting. Come one in, Christi. It's safe."

Meeting? I thought.

He was a short, fat, and balding ex-wrestler; somewhat typical of the leaders of many institutions of public education. He was kind of ugly for a pretty lady like Christi. Wow, she was all right. Christi, the secretary, who always made me shake when I asked her for another book of library passes; who always gave such exciting, hello-fella smiles when I asked for extra report card forms. Christi of the wonderful body, Christi of the tight skirts and revealing blouses. I had a desk full of passes and unused report cards.

"Oh, Mr. Vincent, do you think we ought to take a chance like this?"

"Nothing to worry about, baby. It's safe here. Those long-winded bastards in the English Department can never meet for less than an hour."

He stumbled over a chair, cursed, and turned on the lights so he could see. She closed the door and then they passionately embraced. He was holding her in his chubby arms and kissing her sweet mouth. She gently caressed his thick neck with her small hands and, between kisses, mumbled sexy sounds into his cauliflower ears.

He backed her up against the shelf. My shelf.

"Oh, Mr. Vincent, we shouldn't be doing this at school."

"Want me to stop, baby?"

"Of course not, silly," she giggled.

And, while they whispered sweet nothings and touched each other's nasty places, my mind screamed, "Mantra, mantra, mantra," but my eyes were open and her magnificent ass was pressed deeply into the narrow gap between the sophomore lit books and *Fifty Great American Short Stories*.

It still kind of heats me up thinking about her, Newfriend.

But, to continue...there were also enlightening times that occurred in my invisible realm of the book room.

While transfixed and becoming the cool, spring air that swept down through the depths of some imagined green valley, I heard a colleague tell another, "Watkins' beard looks like a maggot's nest."

And then, in a get-out-of-the-garden-you-apple-eating-sinner's voice, the darkness behind the bookshelf rang out with, "Better in the beard than up the nose, Mother."

Invisible times they were. I never intended on eavesdropping. I wouldn't do that on purpose. A better way of describing the situation is like one day when I was meditating and a mouse walked across my foot and nibbled at my shoelace. It must have sensed that I was alive but it didn't react to me at all. See what I mean? Regardless of how intensely we are perceiving the world, silence can make us invisible.

And, of course, in a world without bullshit there is a great deal of silence.

Chapter Seven
Ham and Love on Rye

Silence is not necessarily non-communicative, though. It's just that when encountering silence and invisibility it becomes necessary to listen and look more deeply. It's rare when we bother to do so.

Interesting, isn't it, my friend? In a mystical sense, the closer we get to actualizing the inner core of our being, our Zen-ness, that which is one with the entire Universe; the more we seem to cease to exist on the plane of normal intercourse. My mother used to say there were days when she felt like crawling in a hole and pulling the hole in after her. I wonder if she was talking about Nirvana.

I'll tell you a quick "silence" story and then we'll ditch the philosophy and get on with the plain and painful truth of events.

It was Paris back a few years ago when life was considerably lighter that it is now. Maureen and I had been traveling around Europe on Eurail passes. Paris was outdoor cafes and summer-green sidewalk trees all rain-puddle-reflected and very much the Impressionist's painting we had sought. We were still in that blissful stage of a relationship when there is more laughter than bickering. There was a gentle, easy beauty about those days of lusting and laughing. Such an adventure it was.

We were riding one of the old subway lines, rumbling down through the bowels of the under-city, peering out the windows into the caked darkness expecting to see some guy in a mask playing an organ. The car was crowded and filled with vousez-vous chatter neither of us could understand. We weren't sitting together. Maureen had a regular seat but the only place left for me was this little fold-down platform hanging on the wall next to one of the doors. We were just jostling along and I was making faces at her through the arm-and-elbow gaps of the standing crowd and she was smiling glimpses back at me when we came to a stop. Through the door windows I saw a lady out on the platform with her arms full of packages. The old-style cars had latches on the doors that had to be turned before they would slide open. From my spring-loaded chair I could see she didn't have a free hand and in a sweep of graciousness I stood and released the latch for her from the inside. Then I sat back down on the space where the seat would have been had it not, with the momentary absence of my mass upon it, sprung back to its upright position. I hovered there for an instant and then, with a less than gracious shout of "Whoa!" crashed mightily to the floor.

The train lurched forward.

Maureen, catching sight of her beloved sprawled upon the rushing floor, seeing the shuffling French-folk trying to avoid stepping on this Ugly American, and the slapstick attempts he made to rise from the shifting scene, cut loose with a grand hoot and crackle of laughter that rattled the world. Laughter that was only quelled by her self-conscious awareness that, save the rumble and whoosh of the rolling subway, it was the only sound in the car.

It became dead silent and everybody except Maureen looked away. I grabbed a bar and got up. A pretty little girl peeked over her mother's shoulder and grinned at me but was immediately spun about and chided for the indiscretion. Maureen and I just looked sheepishly at each other and were thoroughly relieved when populations shifted at the next stop and people started talking again.

Someone could have said, "Vousez-sorry you busted your ass-a-vous." But no one did. You see, in the silence so much more was said than ever could be spoken by polite patter. In the silence I realized the centuries of that ancient city—through the horrors of plagues, the devastation of wars, the oppression of despots—had taught the Parisians not laugh at the misfortune of others. And, by the averted attention of the crowd, I learned it was proper for one to be given opportunity to regain one's dignity without fear of mocking scrutiny.

You see, Newfriend? I landed on my buns on Level 1 and the French people spoke their reaction on a much higher and purely non-verbal level.

Let's get back to the telling of today's tale.

After my head had healed for a few days, Wes, my English teacher buddy, drove me home from the hospital.

"Thank you for the ride home from the hospital, Wes, my friend. Don't forget you are thirty-two and only have twenty-three more years to go before you can retire."

"Thank you, Greg. I'll go right home and think about that."

"Perhaps you can start putting a little money away now, from time to time, for that nice fishing pole you'll be needing then."

"Greg."

"What?"

"Maybe I'd better run you back up to St. Ferd's. I don't think they finished fixing your head."

"Thanks, Wes, but I believe I'll try it on the outside for a while. Some things can't be fixed."

He laughed and drove away. Wes is a good man. He's really going to miss me.

I was still slightly dizzy, but the headache was gone and, after all it was spring and I didn't have to return to work for a few days and..."My God," I said aloud. "Maureen's gone. Nobody is home. The place will be empty."

I sat down on the concrete step in front of the apartment house. It was a big old house that had been converted from a meeting hall for some fraternal organization to a building housing five apartments. The doors were eight feet high and made of dark heavy wood.

I sat and watched the cars and trucks. There were no buses. This town is too small for regular bus routes. My mind rambled in futile avoidance of the sickness of dread. The forsythia bushes had already passed their prime and the broad-leafed trees were pale green with new leaves. Sunlight was shaded from the porch all day. The step was chilly, as if it didn't know that spring had happened. "Look at the beer can in the hedge," I said.

Sometime later (perhaps minutes; perhaps hours), I entered the lobby and opened my mailbox. There was nothing important: a few bills, an advertisement for lawn fertilizer, and another note from Fred the Killer who always wrote the same message:

Dear Gregory,

    I'm going to smash your head with a brick and chop your balls off with a meat cleaver and run you over with a big ugly truck, damn you.

                Love,
                  Fred the Killer.

"Oh." I said.

I had never minded being alone before. It was usually good for me to be by myself. The thought of an existence involving only the sounds and motions I desired had always appealed to me, especially at school with the bustle of a thousand kids or at home with Maureen telling me what a bastard I had become. But, somehow, the thought of entering that lonely apartment depressed me so much I could barely force myself to climb the stairs. Trying to console myself, I thought, there won't be any dripping panty hose to trickle water down my neck when I lean over to turn on the shower. "It will be quiet," I said. Quiet, which had once been craved, turned about and now was feared.

So this is life with a broken head, I thought.

The hall looked like a whorehouse in an old cowboy movie. The woodwork was dark and highly polished. The stairs were covered with soft carpet; on the walls was red wallpaper embossed with patterns of tactile fuzz.

The light was off at the top of the stairs. It didn't come on until dark and, consequently, I had difficulty finding the keyhole.

So quiet. Only the sound of my searching key.

Then....

"Surprise!"

The door was flung open revealing a room filled with streamers and posters with sayings like: "Welcome Home, Greg" and "Watch Out for Your Head" and, my favorite, "Do You Want a Poached Egg, Greg?"

Someone turned up the radio and it started blasting wild music. A hand reached out and shook mine, "Come on in, Greg. You're holding up the party."

It was Melvin.

The rest of the party consisted of Maureen.

Maureen always tried so hard for me. Even toward the end of it all she kept trying. The sad part of it was how her efforts started missing the mark. Somehow I knew it would have been foolish to try to correct that kind of miscalculation.

I'll give you an example of how things were and how they changed.

She used to put so much love into my lunches.

Since I had been a little kid in the first grade, I always took my lunch to school. The monotony of peanut butter and jelly sandwiches being preferable to the torture of green beans. I hated green beans back then and it seemed like there was a huge portion of them on every school lunch plate that I had bought during first grade. If you didn't eat all of your green beans, you had to stay in the lunchroom until you sneaked all of them into your pockets or the bell rang ending lunch period.

By the end of my first month of school, I was starting to grow pale from lack of sunlight and exercise during lunch hour. I was only able to pocket the beans on one occasion and got caught leaving the cafeteria. When I stood up one had squeezed halfway to freedom and was leering out at the teacher.

I told Maureen this sad tale soon after we were married and for years she tried to make lunch a special occasion for me.

Instead of bologna on white bread with a Twinkie, I would get kosher corn beef on Russian pumpernickel with lettuce, tomato, and sliced pickle and an insulated cup of homemade soup with croutons on the side.

At times, the extent of her efforts proved to be an embarrassment to me.

When I was going to night school and working days in factories, I always tried to eat my lunch away from the other employees because, as soon as it was discovered that my lunches were spectacular acts of love, I became a sideshow attraction to everybody in the plant.

The big, greasy, factory guys would stand around gawking and saying things like, "Gee, Marvin, I wonder what taste delight Gregory is going to ingest today?"

There was a time when I went unnoticed for several weeks until my lunch box fell open on the way back to the machines and a sterling silver napkin ring rolled out.

In one factory, I think it was the Swellbee Brothers Steel Door Plant, we would eat our lunch in a loft where cardboard boxes were stored. It was cleaner and warmer up near the ceiling. After working there a couple of months the novelty of my lunches had just about declined to casual glances over my shoulder by a few friends rather than a huge crowd of near-strangers milling around the factory rafters.

I reached into my black lunch pail and thought, Looking good—three slices of lean ham, Swiss cheese, lettuce, tomato and pickle on rye.

I opened up the sandwich to add the tomato, which, of course, was wrapped separately so as to keep the bread dry, and my friend, Jack, the factory worker, poked my side and said, "Hey, Greg, that ain't no pickle. It's a ten-dollar bill."

Sure enough, there was a ten-dollar bill folded up to look just like a long, thin slice of pickle—even the ends were somehow rounded.

I unfolded the bill and there was a note inside which, with considerable pressure from my co-workers, I read aloud:

Dear Greg,

I'm sorry, but I was out of pickles so I thought you and your friends might like to stop for a couple of beers after work.

Love,
Maureen

"Step right up, ladies and gentlemen. Hurry, hurry, hurry."

When I finished my degree and we moved out West, one of the first plans I had as I embarked upon my new career as an educator was to dine in the school cafeteria. I had hated the experiences and sensations of eating in school lunchrooms as a kid. But, no longer a frightened and finicky child and, having suffered so many uncomfortable situations resulting from Maureen's loving lunches (I could never have asked her to tone them down, it would have hurt her feelings), I decided to risk consumption of the plastic-plated fare.

"It will be a good hot meal," I told her as I mustered my courage.

However, the first day of school proved more than I could bear. As I approached the lunchroom and smelled the same vegetable-and-mystery-meat smell that had gagged my youth, I instantly conjured up images of hundreds of kids with green beans squishing around in their pockets. Needless to say, I immediately reversed course mid-hallway, intending never again to enter the facility for purposes of ingesting nourishment.

Within a week, once again, I was a lunchtime celebrity, this time in a faculty lounge.

One more wonderful lunch story and I'll move on.

One evening I was sentimentally sipping a few beers and feeling sorry for myself, and I revealed to Maureen that when I was a kid we almost never had potato chips. I told her I remembered one occasion, though, when we had a giant bag. I was in bed with strep throat at the time. The whole family, except me, sat around eating Dad's big surprise. Dad didn't intend his gift to be cruel, he just didn't think. But Melvin, at great risk of contamination, sat right next to my sick bed and chewed in my ear.

"Crunch, crunch."

As a teacher, I had given up my metal, factory lunch box and used a paper bag, which, unlike several of the more frugal teachers who neatly folded their bags and carried them back home for recycling, I threw away. It wasn't unusual for me to carry my lunch in various kinds of bags from clothing stores, grocery stores, and, also, in bags that had once contained cookies, Fritos, and the like.

That's why I didn't take much notice of the fact that my lunch was in a potato chip bag one day.

The surprise came when I unrolled the top of the bag in front of the usual lunchtime crowd and found it to be completely full of potato chips and, to the "oo's" and "ah's" of a dozen reading over my shoulder, I silently read the note written in large red letters:

Dear Greg,
    Crunch! Crunch!
    I love you.
    Maureen.

You know, she really loved me.

I hate to tell you about the last lunch she packed me a few months ago before I told her to forget it. I guess I deserved it.

"Greg, I haven't checked into you lunch bag lately," someone in the teacher's lounge had said. "Let's see what kind of love-wrought goodies Mama has for you today."

"Oh, it's probably just something simple," I said.

"Let's take a look. Let's take a look," said the edging crowd.

I opened the bag and said, "My, my, a raw turnip. Let me wash the dirt off it and then, by damn, why don't we all just have a nice big feast?"

It started out strained, our little me and Melvin and Maureen party.

At first they just stood there with their eyes and I just stood there with my feet.

"I like the one about the poached egg, Maureen," I said, breaking the silent stalemate.

"I, we...er...Maureen thought someone should be here when you got home from the hospital," said Melvin on the half-laugh. "So, I said, 'What the heck, Maureen, why not, after all, he is still my brother even if I did steal his wife. Right?'"

"What Melvin means is we...we were thinking of you," said pretty Maureen.

"That's real nice," I said, thinking of the poached egg poster. I would have preferred seeing one that read "I Know You Care, Greg" or "Melvin Drowned."

"Yes," I repeated, "I really like the one about poached eggs." And I thought, you're really trying, my love—a little party, posters. You're still trying and missing. Trying and missing.

"So, we just hopped on my multi-million-dollar Leer Jet and flew straight out here. Nothing's too good for my woman. Isn't that right, Maureen?"

"Yes, Melvin," she said quietly.

Wine? Oh, did we drink wine—by the $.99 quart. "For my brother, I only buy the worst," joked Melvin as he laughed and laughed.

Laugh? God, did we laugh. We laughed about what seemed like centuries of funny stuff. We laughed about how Melvin got to kiss Lou Anna Martin right on the mouth back in fifth grade. We laughed about the expression on my face when Melvin was eating the potato chips and I had strep throat. We laughed about how the scant, bikini top to Maureen's swimming suit had come off in the surf just the night before and how her great, big, beautiful breasts had jumped right out in front of one of Melvin's riotous Myrtle Beach, beach parties. We all had tears in our eyes from the laughter. I guess we laughed about everything that ever happened for Melvin or happened to me.

The three of us. Just the good, ole, three of us on the red Mediterranean couch with Maureen in the middle and Melvin and me on the ends.

"I'm sure glad you people showed up. I mean, with Maureen and you crapping on me like you did, it was a pretty bleak prospect to return to this big apartment and find no one here."

"Well, brother, glad to help out in a time of need," said Melvin. "We thought, didn't we Maureen, what the hell, just because I stole your woman from you doesn't mean we all can't be friends. Isn't that right, Maureen?"

"Yes, Melvin. That's right." With that, she slowly turned, stretched her legs across my lap, dropped her head onto Melvin's lap, and passed out.

"You know what, Melvin?" I asked, staring straight out into the living room.

"What's that, Greg, old brother, old pal?"

"I'm a real bastard," I said.

"True, true, true." he said.

"And you know what else, Melvin?" I continued.

"What's that, Greg?"

"You're twice the bastard I am."

And, with a distant, pensive smile, he said, "I know, I know."

I pulled up the bottom of the short skirt Maureen was wearing and rested my hand upon her soft smooth thigh. She stirred momentarily, opened her sweet hazy eyes and, from some ancient repository of unspoiled passion deep within, said, "Oh yes, Greg."

I gently moved around the edge of her white little panties and touched her moist vagina. She moaned slightly.

"Say, Greg, old brother, say what...what are you doing to my Maureen?"

"What did you say, Melvin, you old bastard you?"

"Your hand there. It's...uh..."

"Oh, do you mean this?" I said, nodding toward Maureen's slumbering lap.

"Well, yes."

"Gee, Mel, old buddy brother, I guess I'm finger fucking my wife."

There was a knock at the door.

"Come in," I yelled. "The door's unlocked."

"No!" Melvin whispered.

"Come on in!" I yelled with drunken zeal.

The door swung open and a large young man with a shaved head and wearing a camouflage fatigue jacket marched in aggressively. Under his left arm he carried some official looking papers. I immediately knew he was a process server. He had quite a sight when he looked around the place with the streamers and posters on the walls and empty wine bottles strewn around the floor. Not to mention Maureen lying there across two men, and me with my hand in her shorts.

Melvin jumped up to hide Maureen, flopping her head down on the couch cushion as he rose. Almost landing in the middle of Maureen, he sat down on the edge of the couch right next to me, with my little brother knee slapped tightly against his big brother knee. I think he even put his arm around my shoulder trying to join our bodies into a solid shield for Maureen's virtue.

I said, "Melvin, I didn't know."

He frantically whispered back, "Get your hand out of Maureen's pants, damn you. You're making a fool out of me."

Our visitor's demeanor had shifted from wonder to disgust.

I think I heard Melvin growl.

"Is one of you perverts Gregory Watkins?" he barked.

"That's him there," said Melvin, pointing to me in the same way he did when we were kids and he would jump away from the scene of a crime and gesture at me saying, "He did it. He did it."

Looking into the dull, steel glare of the messenger of doom, I said, "Want some wine?"

"No," he said with the disdain I had sought. "I'm here on official court business."

"Official?" I asked.

"Official," he said. "Gregory Watkins, here are your divorce papers."

And, with an about face and a few goose steps, he was gone.

Slam.

"Divorce papers," I said as I sadly severed intimate caress of my beloved Maureen.

Melvin stood up. He grinned sheepishly at me and said, "Talk about a party pooper."

Maureen woke up.

"Who was that?" she asked.

"The man with the divorce papers," I said.

And then she said something that made me know she had really loved me.

"Oh." she said.

Chapter Eight
Fred the Killer

You're probably wondering about Fred the Killer of whom I made passing reference a few moments ago.

I don't blame you. I've been wondering about him for years.

Chapter Nine
"It ain't all good times and exotic ladies"

I'd best speak a moment here of the philosophy of personal torment: How what is right and necessary can still hurt.

I learned this from an old drinking buddy of mine last week. I'll tell you about it.

Matt's Bar was a dark place to enter from the bright sunlight of a Friday afternoon. Wandering in from the glaring sidewalk into the dim, table-filled room was dangerous. I always feel stupid when I stumble through a crowd of people whose acclimated eyesight enables them to see when I am temporarily blinded. It takes courage to risk the humiliation of limited perception.

But Friday afternoon was a good time to stumble into Matt's Bar for it was hors d'oeuvres time. Matt's had the best happy hour appetizers in town—big chunks of tender beef lying in a pool of spiced gravy, nachos, fancy crackers and slices of cheese, little rolls of ham—such a wonderful free meal if you had the gall and the stealth to make three or four passes at the serving table. A week had passed since my "welcome home" celebration and I was a starving bachelor. The "guests" at my "Welcome Home, Greg" party had left rather abruptly after the arrival of the divorce papers.

"Hey, Greg," came a voice from the darkness. "Come over here before you kick over any more chairs."

Though I couldn't see well enough to distinguish more than shadowy forms, I knew it had to be Ben. He was an insane friend of mine and it was after 4:30, so, in addition to being crazy, he would also be half-drunk. An interesting thing about Ben was that when he drank he would immediately become half-drunk, but, no matter how long the evening's challenge persisted, I don't recall him ever totally succumbing to the debilitating effects of booze.

His wife had left him almost a year earlier, so he was particularly glad to run into me.

"I hear your old-lady ran off to Myrtle Beach with your rich brother," said Ben.

"Yeah, Ben, that's the truth. But I don't really think it's hilarious enough to justify you going into convulsions of laugher."

"Ha, ha...he, ha..." he sputtered, as he slammed his fist on the table, tears filling his eyes and running over and down his red cheeks. "A curse upon you, Watkins," he was finally able to gasp. "You're sober."

"Not so fast, Ben. I just got here."

"That's the attitude, old buddy. Get a few brews pumping through that broken heart of yours and you'll start seeing a little humor in this life."

I let my eyes adjust to the light for a moment and then headed for the bar. "And while you're up," shouted Ben, "I could use another beer, and how about some more of those Swedish meatballs, and...."

I took a long sip from a cold bottle of Budweiser and Ben asked, "Now, isn't that better? Get used to it. All us dumped on, former husbands are drunks."

"Is that right?" I asked, taking a bite of my custom-created taco packed with exotic cheeses, meats, and hot sauces.

"Pretty much. There might be a few exceptions over in Salt Lake City or in Saudi Arabia, but most of the rest of us slosh a few whenever we can."

"If your extensive survey is limited to the two of us, I can't argue with your findings."

"Hell, Greg, you're just a novice," said Ben with a sudden seriousness to his voice. "What's it been? A few days? Wait until you have your first meal at a restaurant where the two of you used to eat all of the time. It can get real hard to swallow, man. Wait until autumn comes by and, for the first time since before you can remember, your wife isn't giving you grief about raking the leaves. Just think of it, Greg. All those crispy fucking leaves and the smell of autumn and your old lady's still gone. Christmas can be a bitch but, for me, it's not too bad; I never liked it much anyway. But New Year's Eve. Goddamn, Greg, New Year's Eve was a tough one this year. We hadn't missed a Moose Club New Year's Eve party in ten years. We would eat and drink and polka and drink and laugh and drink and then go home to start another lousy year. Hell, sometimes it was two or three o'clock the next afternoon before we'd have our first fight. I tried going this past year as a wild and single guy. I walked into that hall without Darlene and saw all the people dancing and laughing and heard the band playing the same stupid songs it had been playing forever and saw the drunken smiles on the miserable faces of couples we used to party with, and, I swear, Greg, it hurt so bad I almost cried. I had to leave."

"But, Ben," I said carefully. I was unaccustomed to encountering this sentimental side of my friend normally suppressed by loud laughter and sarcasm. "When she left you, you said it was the best thing that could have ever happened to you. You were ecstatic. You even laughed harder about your wife taking off than you did about mine. Isn't that true?"

"Hell, yes! I couldn't stand the bitch."

"Then why...."

"Why do I sit here getting teary-eyed and sentimental over a broad whose most pleasant words in the past decade were, and I quote directly from a very clear memory, 'Well, at least you've got a dick, even if you don't know how to use it.' Why do I suffer for the loss of a woman who had premenstrual syndrome 365 days a year, 366 on leap years? Come on, Greg. You remember Darlene. She hated my guts, along with you and anybody else I dared to call a friend. The only reason we ever got married in the first place was because of too much sloe gin and a broken rubber. And the only reason we stayed together for nineteen years was so she could give her precious little Ben, Jr. a proper home life so that on his eighteenth birthday he could run off to San Francisco with some goddamned coiffeur named Mr. Erikk, with two friggin' "k's."

"Then why do you and so many of us other divorcees drink so much? Why are you so sad when you talk about the passing of seasons and holidays without the company of a woman who treated you like dirt?"

"I guess I miss her."

"Like a toothache?"

"No, like an old habit. Smokers know that cigarettes are deadly but we keep lighting them up. Every day. When you live in the same house with a woman for over two decades, you establish certain patterns. When I'd stumble in the front door at three in the morning, I knew she'd be raising hell, but, I also knew she'd be there. There was usually food on the table in the evening. She was a terrible cook. Somehow when she prepared meat I never quite got over the thought that it was a product of the death of a beast but, by damn, the food was there when I sat down to try to eat it. So when I was hungry I got fed. When I was tired there was always a couch where I could lie down. There was a basement where I could hide from her, a garage where I could comfortably waste time. And, every now and a distant then, we would buy a bottle of sloe gin—even if I didn't know what to do with my dick."

"So you drink."

"So we drink."

"One more round, please," I said to the passing cocktail waitress.

"Why not? It's got to be better than hitting yourself in the head with a lamp, ay, Greg?" And then he laughed so loudly that it became impossible to be inconspicuous about making return trips to the table of hors d'oeuvres.

You know, Newfriend, Ben was right. Every part of my being that had been encountering Maureen for all those years—through good, bad, or indifferent times, regardless—was empty at her loss.

And it hurt. It still does.

Or, as Ben concluded about this life of a bachelor, "Well, I'll tell you what, Greg. It ain't all wild times and exotic ladies."

Chapter Ten
"This is Millie, you bastard."

So we ate what little free food we could sneak and drank some beer and then I went home and tried to sleep.

I was thinking about Maureen. About how there were nights when I would just touch her shoulder and she would awaken and flow into my arms and kiss me with her warm lips. And I thought about how her panties and tee shirt would pull away and how she would open to me and how I would glide within the hot excitement of her manifest desire and....

I was thinking about Maureen and I couldn't sleep. A dozen beers and still I couldn't sleep.

I couldn't sleep until the gray light of early morning when exhaustion prevailed over the torture of memory.

Ring.
The phone.
Ring...ring...
Get the phone. It was six o'clock in the far and sleepy morning of the night of no sleep.

I groggily sorted the clutter of the nightstand and found the receiver.

Ring.
I had been thinking of Maureen. I said out loud to the lonely bedroom, "Maureen?"

I grabbed the phone.
"Maureen?" I asked.
"Maureen...hell, no. This is Millie, you bastard."
"Millie?"

I've put off telling you about Millie. I feel kind of guilty about Millie. The nice way to put it is that I had an affair with her. I could try to explain it away as a product of my

67

desperation or justify it by the realization my wife had been sleeping with my brother for God knows how long.

But the fact is I cheated on my wife. And the fact is in doing so I made love with a woman to whom I could never give my heart. That's wrong, Newfriend.

Millie was beautiful. She was warm and loving, always ready for me when I needed her and easy to find during the final, bitter period of my marriage. She heard me when I was quiet. I heard her when I was lonely. We heard each other when we were horny.

Okay.

So, it hasn't been all innocence with me. So, I'm not just another hapless victim of the capricious whims of a heartless woman–just a good guy gotten by a gal gone wrong.

I never said I was.

Millie helped me when I needed help.

It all sounds so poetic. Yes, innocent and poetic.

She helped me.

Hell, she did me.

I did her.

We did the deed.

Now, that is poetic.

You probably wonder why I don't have her here with me instead of you. It's funny but I can't see her again now that Maureen has left.

Millie started as an extension of my relationship with Maureen. A tangent from her. A reaction to Maureen; not against her. Millie was a flying buttress to my male ego while Maureen drifted toward Melvin and found fewer and fewer reasons to admire me. I don't think Maureen suspected anything was going on. Millie and I were careful. I suppose some would say sneaky.

That's how it started. But, oh, how it escalated from there. No offence to Maureen, it really had nothing to do with her at all. It didn't lessen my affection for her or how much she excited me. But, I did come to really like Millie. I still do.

There's the answer. That's why I don't have her here with me now.

I care.

And no matter how desperately I've needed a woman over these last weeks, I haven't called her once. Ain't I a decent fellow.

God! She was good.

I mean Maureen was great—just ask Melvin (the bastard).

But there was something unique in the way Millie and I loved, the way we made love.

We never gave love; we stole it.

We stole it and it was burning hot ("...like a ring of fire...")

One morning earlier this spring, before the final collapse, Maureen had left for work and I ran into Millie on the sidewalk in front of the apartment. Right out the window there. We just grinned the secret language of sinners and headed straight upstairs. In the excitement of the moment, I couldn't find the key to the front door of the apartment.

So, we did it right there on the carpeted landing between apartment #3 and apartment #4.

That's how wild it was with us. Right on the rug. The old lady living in #3 never said anything about it, but she hasn't seen me since without giving me the damnedest grin.

I know. There goes the sympathy. No more, "Woe to poor old Greg, mistreated saint."

I don't care. I must tell the truth.

Melvin agrees that I'm a bastard, and he's always right about everything. You can ask him.

It's just that I don't think things would have gone so far if it weren't for the way Maureen gave up on me over these last couple of years.

Or maybe they would have anyway.

I don't know. There's no point in trying to blame anyone. There's nothing to gain from it.

So, Millie woke me up that morning two weeks ago saying, "Damn you, Greg. Your wife's been gone for days and you haven't even called me."

"Yeah, I know, Millie. Believe me, you've been on my mind but, somehow, I haven't been able to do much of anything. None of this has been easy. Please, don't hate me, Millie. You haven't done anything wrong. It's me. I'm still kind of screwed up. I haven't gotten any of this worked out yet."

"But I miss you, Greg."

There was a pause. Me looking for words to explain what I couldn't say; her trying to say the words she knew she had to say.

"You're wearing your pink flannel nightgown with flowers all over it, aren't you, Millie? The one that I would slip so smoothly over your head and make you naked."

"Yes, Greg."

"I can see you. God, Millie, it hurts to look, you're so pretty."

There was another pause.

"Do you mean 'goodbye?'" she said.

Then came the longest pause of all with her waiting to hear the words that would have made a future possible and me desperately but hopelessly trying to say them, but not being able to say them. When I would go to her with my ego bruised and my skivvies aflame, it was with honest lust. But then Maureen was gone. Millie deserved more and I couldn't honestly give it to her. At this point in my life, physical love is bullshit.

"Goodbye, Greg," she said and hung up.

Chapter Eleven
Interlude: Truth

I've told you the truth about Millie. Now, I suppose it time that I tell myself the truth about Maureen.

It might seem that I'm blaming all this on honesty. Maureen left me because I couldn't honestly express my vast love for her in the trivial terms she needed to hear. Yes, I'm sure it was purely for a lack of small talk on my part that she chilled to my touch and locked loins with Brother Melvin. (Jeez, Newfriend. What an insult that is. I mean, if Maureen had run off, say, with my friend Wes, the English teacher, or some other worthy male whose lusty whims might have overlooked the formality of her being my wife, I might understand. But Melvin....)

Possibly the most difficult aspect of this curse of honesty with which I live is that I must be as forthright with myself as I am with the rest of the world. There is such a difference between theories of life and their application.

I might be a crazy old "Mariner" but I'm not stupid. The truth is, Maureen didn't quit loving me, and she just lost interest in someone with whom she shared less and less life. As hard as it is to admit, my brother-in-law, Herbert, in the whine of his bumpkinesque blather had said it right. How did he put it? Oh, yes. I can hear it now, "You quit doin' all the stuff that makes life more-n-a god blasted junkyard."

I might have been quitting on life long before life quit on me.

You know, we never did make babies, Maureen and I. Instead, we made excuses about careers and travel and other fleeting priorities. "Perhaps later," we would say. "After we've seen the Leaning Tower of Pisa." I've never dared to let this thought crystalize before this very moment, Newfriend. I've avoided confronting it, but I think we never made babies because I never truly committed myself to either my marriage or, in a larger sense, to life itself—at least not sufficiently enough to risk creating a new human being. What deeper commitment can one have to a marriage that to purposely dedicate it to a child?

I never could make such a commitment, perhaps neither could she. And now she's gone.

Chapter Twelve
Bang

I sat on the edge of the bed listening to Millie's dial tone for a while, then I, too, hung up.

I walked into the kitchen and fried an egg in butter and put it on a piece of bread.

I didn't eat it. I just left it sitting there on a saucer on top of the stove.

I put on my Saturday clothes and stared into the empty space left in the closet where once hung the bright-colored party dresses, the serious business dresses and slacks, the blouses with dipping necklines and sweaters that clung.

I thought about Millie and it hurt to deny her but I had no choice. As I've told you, Newfriend, I am a tragically honest man.

I thought about the girl I had met at the English teacher convention, Amy, and the walk around the duck pond. "No help," I said.

I thought about Maureen some more. It might seem that I only think about the sexual facets of our relationship—her clothes, her body, taking off her clothes, making love with her. It's true. Sex is the highest form of physical identification between loving people. It's the easiest part of her to remember. The internal love, the support, the soul sharing: hey, those invisible essences are a lot more gone than the tangible heat of it all. When the heart part of love is taken away you can't think about it. It's too much to handle.

So I think about the vagina parts of love and the penis parts of love and come up with a needed recollection and a bearable pain.

I thought about Maureen some more and reached for an ominous looking box with a padlock on it that was high up on the top shelf of the near-empty closet and out of sight.

I felt around until I located it and dragged it down. It was dusty.

I searched the drawers of the nightstand and eventually located the key.

I unlocked the grey box and took out a great, ugly, metallic-black pistol that had been given to me by an Eastern paranoiac friend years before.

I didn't like the gun. I had shot it at beer cans on one occasion and in brief moments had spent a small fortune on ammunition. It was very loud. My ears rang for hours afterward. It made terrible holes in the beer cans.

Maureen was afraid to have it in the house so I told her I would lock it up in the metal box and hide it somewhere where she would never have to think about it. I put it on the top shelf and gave it little thought until the morning of Millie's call and the near-empty closet.

I stood there in the bedroom holding the gun. It was heavy and cool and powerful.

I rolled open the door to my side of the closet. There were my two teacher sport coats, a few teacher dress shirts and pairs of teacher dress pants, and a rack of clip-on teacher ties—not much there at all. I pulled a tan sport coat from a hanger and put it on.

I put the gun in the coat pocket and walked to the mirror mounted on the bathroom door. I had always secretly wanted to be a private detective like the guys on television.

I ripped the pistol from my pocket and said, "Bang!" and the apartment said, "Echo."

I noticed my face wasn't laughing in the mirror so I took off the coat and went back to the metal box in the bedroom.

I loaded the clip with one very expensive, very deadly cartridge. I rammed the clip back into the butt of the grip. I pulled back the slide and let it snap forward, loading the bullet into the chamber and cocking the pistol.

Then....

Guess. Come on, Newfriend. What did I do?

You'll never guess.

Did I catch a plane to Myrtle Beach and shoot Melvin?

Did I shoot Maureen?

Did I shoot myself and you're sitting here listening to the tirades of a ghost?

Do I still have the bullet in the gun and I'm going to shoot you because you are a wedding guest and I hate anything that reminds me of marriage?

Wrong!

I said you'd never figure it out.

I walked into the kitchen and put the loaded pistol into the vegetable bin of the refrigerator.

PART TWO

School Days and Parties

Chapter Thirteen
Ring

So, we have finished off love. Let us move on to the other sources of my cynicism: my career and my friends. These two elements of a dwindling life force are intertwined.

I am, or, rather, was a schoolteacher and most all of my friends, or, rather, ex-friends are schoolteachers. I'll explain the social dynamics of this incestuous phenomenon later when I tell you about teacher parties. First, though, I'll give you a couple of the highlights of my professional experience that are pertinent to the bitter truth of this Saturday morning.

As I said, I used to be an educator. Actually, until yesterday I was a high school English teacher. I'll tell you about how a teacher without the communicative protection of bullshit gets himself in trouble.

It all gets mixed up from here on—marriage, friends, jobs. These elements sometimes even seem disorganized to me. But today they have all my focus and I am depending upon the fact that there will be a sense of order in their completion.

There has to be.

I've told you about my busted head and busted marriage, now I'll tell you about my busted career.

Ringgg...

Here he comes. School bell's a-ringin', school's a-startin: Here come the teacher, here come the teacher.

> School rooms are ice trays,
> the students are cubes:
> Some grow their whiskers;
> some grow their boobs.

It was about two months ago and I was conferring with the principal of my school concerning a class I was teaching. "Watkins, that reading class you're teaching is too easy. The kids are saying it's a crip course. They all want to take it."

"Oh." I said.

I had known something was going on that morning when there was a genuine, hand-written note in my box along with the yellow roll cards and the stack of photocopied memos listing which students were to be excused for what sporting events. It's funny how you know when something bad is coming.

Hear the laughter?

I've always been frightened of authority figures— policemen, teachers, bosses, school secretaries, license bureau clerks, women in general, etc. and Mr. Vincent, principal of the high school, provided me no respite from that fear. He was gruff and sour and had spoken friendly words to me on only one occasion in the two years I had worked in his building. On that occasion he queried my reaction to a Denver Bronco's football game and I shattered any chance of finer rapport with the man by uttering something like, "What football game?"

His reaction was, "You gotta be kidding." and then he just walked away, shaking his head in disbelief.

That was the only friendly greeting he ever gave me— an occasional nod, but never a smile.

The note that morning read:

> Watkins, be in my office during your conference
> period today.
> > Mr. Vincent.

Sometimes I wondered if his mother named him "Mr."

The manner in which a school administrator pays his or her highest compliment to professional educators is by ignoring them completely, except, of course, in informal discussions concerning sporting events and the skyrocketing price of lawn fertilizer.

The note made me nervous.

"...They all want to take it," he had said.

A course entitled "Individualized Reading" should endeavor to foster in students a sense of self-motivation regarding reading. In such an affective realm as attitudinal manipulation, the students' personal preferences in reading material should be respected and given credit toward satisfying the requirements of the class, as specified by the qualitative guidelines delineated by the School District's "Instructional Criteria for the Language Arts Curriculum."

Pretty good, huh? That's what a "real" teacher would have told the principal in defense of his position. You throw around a few terms like "motivation," "criteria," "attitudinal," and "affective," and you can get away with saying almost nothing and sounding professionally profound at the same time. If I had rattled off a crock of educational rot, Vincent would have said, "Yeah..." and I would have been out of his office in minutes and upstairs eating my conference period orange without a hitch.

But, you see, when you have meditatively extracted deceit from your communicative bag of tricks, ass-kissing is next to impossible.

I didn't want to confront the man. I told you that by the nature of his position he generically frightened me—but I wasn't capable of lying to him either.

So, I began, "If students think my reading class is easy, then I'd say it's successful."

"Yeah, Watkins, but you're going to have to make it harder. You know—required reading lists, page number requirements, uh, book reports. You know what I mean—like when we were in school. Harder. Make it look better. The way you've got it now it's like some kind of a goddamn recess. And the things they're reading—I get calls every day from parents asking me what the hell is going on with their kids reading The Happy Whore for an English class."

"Hooker, sir."

"What?"

"Hooker. The book is titled *The Happy Hooker.*

"I don't give a damn if it's The Wholesome Harlot. It doesn't belong in a school and nobody should get academic credit for reading such smut."

I couldn't help myself. I laughed out loud. "Wholesome Harlot, that's a good one, Mr. Vincent. Ha, ha, ha..."

"Yeah, that wasn't too bad, was it?" he said, and we went "ha, ha, ha " for a while together before I interrupted the merriment and shocked us both.

"But, you know what, Mr. Vincent, you're full of bologna."

"What did you say?"

"I guess I said you're full of bologna. I mean, you administrators let teachers design a class called 'Individualized Reading' and then, with the first hint of controversy coming from one irate parent, you want to throw out the 'Individualized' part of the concept for the whole course." I was on a roll by then. It almost seemed like I was sitting there listening to someone else speak with such blunt honesty. "I'm sick of you chicken-shit principals and your wimping out to the almighty hot-air of a handful of Puritan-assed parents. For once, why don't you think about what's best for our students rather than what's best for district public relations?"

"Jeez, Watkins, have you ever been a jock?"

"No. Why?"

"You English teachers don't use language like that."

"Yeah, that wasn't too bad, was it?" I said.

"You're fired," he said.

"Oh." I said.

That was the end of our conference but not my career. I wasn't fired. The thought was sincere enough, but the process was too much trouble to carry out. Having completed three full years of teaching, the educator is given tenure. Tenure is a mass of red tape that makes it a real bother to get rid of a teacher who has committed any offence which can be enacted while wearing clothes.

But I'm getting this too much out of order. You could become confused.

My teaching career began an old junior high school where I experienced what I refer to as "The Inquisition." Following that trial, I moved on to Forker Middle School where modern education intersected with political intrigue. The past two years I've been at the local high school under the direction of the above-mentioned Mr. Vincent. (Remember Mr. Vincent, Newfriend? That's right. He was the guy in the book room with the pretty secretary.)

I'll try to get this back into chronological order. I'm trying to be a thoughtful storyteller but it's difficult. Life may seem to be chronologically developed from birth to death, but such order is illusion. The sequential ordering of time is always contrived. Einstein says time is just a wrinkled up rubber sheet anyway—all stretched out, bumpy and warped by mass. It's like this story. Everything is known at the same instant, or, really, non-instant, since time is a joke. Right now I know the whole story—the whole story exists but I have to feed it to you in small bites so as to avoid choking you. Life—years, days, moments—is the same. We can only take small increments of it at the same time…so we don't choke.

How do I know the essence of time when so many others delude themselves with notions of the immutable truth of Rolex watches? Don't worry about it. I probably don't know anything.

I'll start several years ago with an event I have come to call "The Inquisition."

I was my first teaching job. I worked at a junior high school exposing students to the rudiments of English grammar and composition. Exciting days. Comma days, subordinate clause days. Red ink days. Days of long duration, short pleasure, and little justification.

I'll tell you the stories in this part of my tale because they show the kinds of forces that have been acting upon me over these years and have helped, as I said, create the essence of this day.

I'm not trying to impress you with the cruelty and deviousness of our fellow human beings or with the horrors of modern education. It's just the story I know, the one that manipulated me into this late Saturday morning with its sunshine and impatience.

This is my story. One element that makes it significantly different from your story or the stories of a million others is the fact that very soon it will be complete. The living world dangles for tomorrow. I can tie a neat little string around my package and call it finished—not because of my bitterness, not because of the severing effects of hatred, not because of some exceptional gift of prophecy enabling me to see more clearly and distantly than the rest of you. Once I am through articulating this simple tale of woe, there will be no problem gathering the diverse facets of a life package: My package will be completely empty.

Junior high schools are strange places. The students are at various stages of sexuality and, generally, are perverted. The seventh graders draw nasty things and think nasty things, the eighth graders are nasty things, and the ninth graders do nasty things. When they assume their many defensive postures during passing periods between classes, it looks like an invasion of huge grasshoppers with all their arms and legs. Sometimes when the girls come up to your desk to have their compositions checked, they will bump their fresh little parts against your elbow and not even know where the good feeling is coming from. The careful and non-pedophilic teacher quickly learns to build a fortress of desk drawers around himself.

A teacher has to be careful.

Eighth graders are the worst. They are about thirteen years old and, while they don't have as much gas as the seventh graders or as much arrogance as the ninth graders, their hormonally twisted psyches abound with a vast quantity of a much more despicable commodity: cruelty. Their favorite word is "retard."

However, for the many months of four long school years I molded minds in junior high and, each night, I would wash my hands like after a practical joke that has the punch line, "Yeah, but your cup wasn't full of piss."

It wasn't all bad. Most of it wasn't bad at all. There were good times, moments of communication when shadowy figures haunted their darting eyes with depth and distance. Moments of humor when the drudge of our days together would thunder in good laughter. Moments when their stretching, extending bodies would pause their frantic motions and honestly think and feel.

I just hated the ruthlessness and the spit wads. The humanity I didn't mind at all.

But I'm going to tell you about a bad time. Stories about bad times last longer.

I've got to tell this. It was long before I learned to meditate, back in the days when I was still struggling with the ineptitude of normal conversation—in the silent days before the silence.

It's a story about the dangerous and desperate powers of weak people in a conspiracy of defense against invincible foes. It's about the misspent energies of a group of teachers trying to superficially deal with the mind of an eighth grader.

It's about cruelty and hopelessness.

"Sit down, Mr. Watkins."

"Sure, Mr. Birch." I didn't want to be there. It was the second afternoon in a row that I had been assigned to fill in for a member of the Faculty Discipline Committee and, after the first session, I was disgusted at the sadistic weakness of my colleagues and at the gutlessness of myself.

"Not back there, Mr. Watkins. Up here in front of the committee."

"In front?"

"Right up here," repeated Mr. Birch.

Mr. Birch was a super-right-wing, racist, sexist, hate-filled, self-righteous, vociferous bastard. And, worse than all of that, he was bigger than me. He was partially bald and totally bigoted. Due to an injury he suffered while serving in the navy during the Korean Conflict, he proudly walked with a limp and carried a menacing cane. Whenever he frowned his way down the hallway the kids would all say, "Oh, no, here come Mr. Birch."

Whenever I would see him heading down the hall I would think, Oh no, here come Mr. Birch.

And there was another disturbing element of his personally. Regardless of the aforementioned catalog of character disorders, he was a "good-ole-boy." If you happened to be male, white, shorthaired, and willing to listen to his daily pronouncements about the doom and contamination of our culture; he could be a hell of a nice guy.

He hated my guts.

This is not going to be pleasant, I thought as I made my way through the semi-circle of teachers and took a seat on the wooden chair in front of the group.

No one spoke and as I sat down the sound of me scooting the chair barked starkly in the ancient classroom creating an audible bruise. There was no humor in the room.

(Life has taught me that though, at times, existence can be filled with sorrow or misery, can seem cruel or even vindictive, it is never serious. Once we cease to be able to laugh, we are no longer capable of considering hope.)

Let me introduce the priests of institutional law and order: the self-appointed tribunal that regularly doled out justice to the most blatant sinners of the student body and, in my case, transgressors in the faculty. I'll describe them as I saw them that day with me sitting in the hot seat and them turning up the heat.

Herbert Lice: A spineless fellow. Lover of other people's small and great misfortunes. Often found hovering in the company of Mr. Birch and, when in Mr. Birch's company, always found nodding his head up and down and muttering such appropriate phrases as, "Kennedy got what he deserved," and, "Martin Luther King got what he deserved," and, of course, the ever adaptable, "It's those damned liberals." (Smiling)

Mrs. Hudson: Possessor of a most pleasant and antiseptic smile. Her eyes glowed and her voice was soft when she said, "Good morning." Her eyes glowed and her voice was soft when she said, "Dirty Mexican." (Always smiling)

Mr. Conway: A good man, just misguided, perhaps naive; hardly sadistic enough to be a junior high school teacher, much less, a standing member of the Discipline Committee. (Not smiling)

Mrs. Days: A stupid, insensitive, semi-innocuous flake. (Smiling vacantly)

Mr. Tumble: A man of a thousand hands, most of them on the wrong people's asses. A goodly, church-going person who knew exactly what to do with bad people. (Smiling)

Mr. Garf: The school disciplinarian. A man who had gained infinite satisfaction from the sound of a flat board slapping violently against the posterior of a wrong-doer and whose life was utterly frustrated by trends less sympathetic to corporal punishment. Very quiet. (Probably had never smiled in his life)

Mr. Drake: A collector and disperser of nigger-spic-gook-et-al jokes, a man for whom huntin'-n-fishin' held considerably more interest than education. Principal of the junior high school. (Smiling a thick smile)

Mr. Birch: The afore-mentioned leader of the pack.

Quite a gathering of humanity, wouldn't you say?

Room 106 in the old school had an ornately decorated plaster ceiling with cracks in it. The Venetian blinds had broken slats. The desks were deeply inscribed with profanity, proclamations of love, and perverted little seventh grader drawings of penises and naked people.

I had gotten into this mess the day before when a mailbox memo had instructed me to fill in on the Discipline Committee for an absent colleague. Hence it was that I joined the inquisitors who had gathered to focus upon a thirteen-year old named Mike: a kid with a baker's dozen years of near-illiteracy, frustration, rejection, and now, this most recent affront: trial by faculty.

He was small. A bone dominated frame with nervous eyes. He was mean as hell, rude, inconsiderate, sassy—a general nuisance to all of his Phase One (low ability) classes. One teacher knew him well and even might have cared for him. She was Mrs. Regis who knew little beyond the confines of the intense classroom where she confronted six small groups of slow readers a day. She didn't know what the committee was or who the committee was. She just knew that Mike was a kid who needed help. When she read the bulletin about the Faculty Discipline Committee, she saw no harm in giving it a try. Mrs. Regis was a kind lady who sincerely wanted to help. As a result of her referral, Mike found himself seated in front of a panel of eight old faces with glaring eyes and sharp tongues and he was scared.

Birch, the huge man with the hard lines and booming voice had begun the proceedings with, "Wipe that smirk off your face, boy!"

Mike jerked and tried to readjust the tense muscles of his face.

Mrs. Hudson started, "Michael, now we know what you're here for—disruptive behavior, talking in class, and insubordination. But can you tell us why you come to school?"

No answer, only a slight shift and eyes to the floor.

"Look at me when I speak to you, young man!" she snapped without losing her smile.

His eyes moved sideways. Up.

"Do you come here to play?"

No answer

"Do you come here to shoot rubber bands?"

No answer.

"Do you come here to visit with your neighbors?"

No answer.

"Answer Mrs. Hudson when she asks you a question, boy!" barked Mr. Birch.

"Do you want a swat?" asked Mr. Garf.

"Yes, tell us, Michael. Why are you in school?" joined Mr. Drake.

Eyes back at the hardwood strips of the floor, he mumbled, "I...I don't know, sir."

"YOU DON'T KNOW?" chorused the Committee. Aghast.

Mr. Lice had heard enough of what the others were saying to have plagiarized an opinion. "Well, just what have you been doing all of these years that you've been wasting a fine education?"

No answer.

"Boy!"

"Nothing, sir."

"NOTHING?"

"What are you talking about, son? 'Nothing,' you say." It was Mr. Tumble. "That's outrageous."

And several of the panel glanced to and fro, rolling their eyes, tsk-ing their tongues, and then, with an uncanny sense of unity, in one great curling wave of indignation they killed him.

Mrs. Hudson: School is not a playground.

Mr. Lice: School is serious business.

Mr. Tumble: School is too valuable to waste.

Mrs. Days: I think...

Mr. Garf: I think he needs a swat.

Mr. Birch: You look up when we're talking to you, boy.

And he looked up.

And tears formed in his eyes and spilled out.

He cried. A tense sob escaped from a choking throat and he cried.

Pride got wet.

And there I was staring out the window with my stomach twisted and my fists clenched, and my goddamned, cowardly mouth clamped shut. I was very quiet.

And I would have remained so. Not the spiritual kind of quiet resulting from meditation; rather, the stomach-knot, high-blood-pressure kind of quiet that comes from the mind-pulping polarity of fear and anger, had it not been for what happened the next morning during my planning period.

I was sitting in the room cluttered with fifteen or so teachers with stacks of ungraded papers before them on the large table or on the laps of those who sat in the easy chairs. There were junk food, open cans of Coke, and conversations about the weather, football, diets, and hatreds. It was a fine group of men and women sitting on couches and chairs nibbling, sipping, and lightly conversing.

Coincidentally, about half of the regular members of the discipline committee were present.

I believe it was Mr. Tumble who started it. "Well, tell me, Watkins, what do you think about the way we handled that little brat yesterday afternoon? I don't think we'll have any more trouble with him. Do you?"

And suddenly a rush of anger overcame its counterbalancing force of social fear within my mind and I blurted, "Yes, Mr. Tumble, I think we will have more trouble with the little brat."

"What?" he said, stunned at my reply to what he had considered to be a question with an obvious answer.

Everyone got real quiet, the nosey bastards. They would yack for years and then at the very moment when I couldn't help but be honest for a few minutes, they all tried their first shot at listening.

Anger had such momentum that it continued. "Yes, we probably will have more trouble with Mike. Before he just hated himself; now he hates us."

"So you don't think we did any good with him yesterday, huh?"

"Not the way you apparently believe you did."

The other committee members in the room stood up and glared at me.

Something of the other voice within me mumbled, "Shut up, you damn fool."

But anger won again when Mr. Lice spoke, "But, Watkins, what's the matter with you? Are you blind?

Didn't you see him bawling? We got to him. We made him cry, Watkins. Don't you understand? We broke him."

"Yeah, I was there, Lice. I saw him cry."

"You can't say we didn't have some effect on the little monster when we made him cry," reasoned Mr. Tumble.

"He hates me, too," I said in a lower tone, which was even more angry.

"Hate?" interjected Mrs. Hudson.

"Yes, hate, Mrs. Hudson." And then all the incomprehensible verbiage of argument exploded my conversation and with words that stamped their feet only to create tiny clouds of dust, I continued. "Thanks to you good people and your magnificent techniques of adolescent psychology, he hates me, too. While you sadists were gloating about your triumph over his face, you probably didn't see beyond the tears and into his eyes."

"Hold on a minute, Watkins," said Mr. Tumble. "What do you mean by calling us sadists?"

"I mean I not only saw his eyes, and they were frighteningly like the eyes of a cornered beast, but I also looked around at your eyes and your faces and I saw the wolfish smiles of your lips and your teeth. You were loving it, loving the destruction."

"Destruction," said Mr. Tumble. "You'd better not talk about us that way. All we were doing is trying to make a decent person out of a social misfit and you make us out to be a lynch mob."

"Well put," I smiled. "A lynch mob."

And then in a general stutter of anger it was quiet for a moment.

Snake-smiling Mrs. Hudson spoke a cruel, well-controlled question, "Well, Mr. Watkins, if you thought the proceedings were so atrocious, then why didn't you speak up yesterday when you could have helped the innocent little child?"

No answer.

"Yeah," said Lice, "If we're so mean why didn't you jump in there yesterday when you could have protected the jerk kid?"

No answer.

A silent stalemate of reason verses anger momentarily locked the movement of my mind.

"He can't even defend himself," said Mrs. Hudson. "No wonder he was of no use to Michael."

And raging, I struck back, "Yes, I can. I didn't speak yesterday because, in my own way, I'm just as much of a coward as the rest of you."

"Oh, really, Mr. Watkins?"

"Really, Mrs. Hudson. The whole process is rotten and I think all of us who participate are sick. You people ban together against a screwed-up little kid and then call yourselves heroes when you make him cry. I sit there scared silent and call myself an idealist. We're all sick. It's no wonder that children like Michael don't have a chance in our world."

"I'm telling Mr. Birch," said Lice as he stormed out of the teacher's lounge.

I was really flying then. With the power of my anger asserting authority over the forces of caution, I spat, "I just hope when that poor kid decides to kill somebody in a few years it's not me." They countered with equal vitriol and I came back with more of the same. This went on for several minutes until we were startled by the volume of our shouting and everyone quit talking and turned away.

That is, everyone except Mrs. Days who never knew exactly was going on anyway. She said, "I think..."

And we all said, "Oh, shut up!"

So there I was, the "inquisitee." All those eyes I had condemned earlier that day were staring at me. With varying poses ranging from synthetic cordiality to the stern countenance of Mr. Garf who, I am certain, would have loved to have given me a swat. Everyone glaring at another sinner to be broken. Everyone except Mr. Conway whom I told you was too nice of a person to be associating with vigilantes. He was staring out the window. I know that window, I thought. I know how you feel, my friend.

Of course, Mr. Birch started. The Committee had been the product of his narrow mind and my attack was a personal matter for him.

I could feel the heat of anger filling my mind. All of the animal defenses were set. All the primordial juices were flowing in anticipation of the assault. All the reasoning processes usurped by instinct.

He said, "Mr. Watkins, it seems you have violated the confidentiality of this Committee. What goes on in this room doesn't belong in faculty lounge discussions."

"Oh, that's great, Birch. What do we have here: a secret society? How very democratic for our fine American junior high school."

Wait.

Newfriend, does all this seem somewhat out of character? I mean I've been describing myself as someone locked within a world of perception with no verbal exits. Maybe you think it is inconsistent that the argumentative fool who fought the Discipline Committee is the same guy who got knocked in the head by his wife for not saying enough.

It's not inconsistent. It's transitional. All this occurred several years ago before I happened upon the depths and isolation of meditation. Before I realized the questionable value of certain kinds of words. Before I was stricken mute in their communication. It was all bullshit. This was back in the time when I believed that there was reason to express a counter-attack to the affronts of the ignorant. Back when I thought a good argument could actually have some value-changing effect on a shallow world. Back before I faced the terrible, lonely truth about communication: It's all bullshit when no one listens. To argue with the ignorant is a paradox. They don't listen: That's why they are ignorant.

I'm not saying I was stupid back then. Just normal.

I could have told this in a more logical manner—the transition, that is. How I progressed from my non-verbal infancy, to my super-verbal adult anger stage, and, finally, back to the non-verbal super-communication that lost me the whole world. But you're already getting bored with this philosophizing. I'll let you off easy.

My times with the Discipline Committee are part of what is wrong with me now. You have to know what it was like. And what I was like back then.

It's all part of what we're waiting for this morning.

I'll shorten this.

The good people of the Faculty Discipline committee climbed all over me and I only fought back once and then shut up for most of the rest of my teaching career.

The people who viciously attacked Michael and later me, they were bad good people. People who felt righteous in the terrible and ignorant things they did. These were, by the petty standards of a world controlled by violence and fear, innocent folk. They live small lives here in this distant community, far from the social excuses of our times such as sprawling cities, poisoned air, rat-crowded tenements, and the like. Even in this idyllic realm of clear-mountain streams and star-filled summer nights there are those who are dark and dangerously afraid.

There is fear everywhere.

There are self-righteous fools everywhere.

What do you think, Newfriend?

And Mike.

What ever happened to that little devil anyway?

Mike, the thirteen-year-old incorrigible rubber band shooter.

Mike, the kid.

You might have read about him in the local newspaper not long ago. He made the paper by trying to kill someone. And, true to form, he screwed it up. He failed to produce death. He was his own target and, predictably, he missed. The bullet passed right through his chest and only made a couple of holes. It never hit anything significant.

He lived.

I was going to go up to St. Ferd's and see him. But, of course, I didn't.

Chapter Fourteen
A Tale from a Far Away Land

I don't want you to think that I am adamantly opposed to education. To the contrary, I believe public education is one of the best institutions of our marvelous, democratic society. If it were not for public schools, mothers would never have the time to learn how to play bridge, shop for new sweaters, or enslave themselves to full-time careers so Little Tammy and Skipper and Big Daddy Dan can live in more than the hovel affordable by Daniel's meager thirty or forty grand a year.

Schools provide a necessary delay in decision making in a young person's life. A dozen years are guaranteed unless Junior or Mary Lou gets caught smoking dope in the main office eleven times and is actually expelled from the ranks of the privileged. Throw in kindergarten, college, and post-graduate degrees, and a person could well be pushing thirty before he or she has to begin playing the real game of life.

Not a bad deal when you think of it.

And also, where in the three-score-and-ten, Biblically-promised years does a boy have more chances to meet girls? A girl more chances to meet boys? (Granted, the chances for life-wrenching rejection are equally magnified in the social intercourse of a public school, but that's the risk of water so deep.)

And sometimes, considerably more frequently than soapbox politicians are wont to admit while attacking the lack-luster leadership of incumbent candidates, an occasional little nipper grows up learning how to read, write, spell, figure, and name the capital of Vermont.

I've seen it happen. Really.

And just hang on a second here, Newfriend. I've got to say this. Let me tell you what actually bothers me about education. It's not the personalities. Jerks like Mr. Birch and Mrs. Hudson are as transient as any mortals to the whims of the gods. Offer them a decent pension or zap them with a 7.5 Richter of a heart attack and they're gone. Just like the rest of us: momentary in our excellence or our menace. Teachers are just like anybody else.

What bothers me most of all is the process of education itself. That's the deadly part. The handling of the fantastic raw material of excited young minds for years until they become apathetic, bulky old minds disguised by school room rituals like staying awake during class and nodding at proper intervals.

I'm an expert on public education. I'm a product of the same machinery. You probably are too, Newfriend.

And it's not just schools. Schools do exactly what they're supposed to do for society. They deaden or desensitize certain portions of the human spirit so as to make us compatible with the demands of the world. The world is a factory; not a studio. The eccentricity that creates severed ears and immortal sunflowers is cracked upon the knuckles at first sign. By lessening an individual's creative and imaginative potential, by discouraging the need to express naked, emotional, tear- and laughter-spoken reactions to sorrow and happiness, by playfully and then seriously conditioning us for the vast majority of boring tasks that fill in the gap from graduation to Social Security, schools prepare us for docile participation in a reality that insults the sacred promise of our entire species.

Whew. Amen. Sermon's over.

But really, what more could a society ask of its school system?

Perhaps it would be appropriate for me to steal a few of our precious moments to relate an ancient fable I discovered while researching my famous undergraduate paper, "The Comma, a Resting Place in a Technological Age."

After all, education has been my life.

I was deep into the eighth-floor stacks of the library of a large Eastern university trying to substantiate the existence of a positive correlation between a student's use of commas and his or her relative seating position in the classroom. I was gleefully thumbing through a thousand-paged treatise entitled Desk Positioning in the American Educational Environment, when I discovered the following tale inscribed in a shaky hand along the margin:

Education: A Myth

Far, far away in a nowhere land. Way up the winding road that climbs the distant sky-mountains, far beyond the mystical city of Wing, beyond the Arker nesting valley of Mug, beyond the Zoda Zoda Sea. I mean really far away, there lived and worked an English teacher.

Aside from the exotic local in which he dwelled, he was just like you and me. He diligently went through the motions of his daily work pattern to use up his many years. You know the type. Just like you and me.

He didn't die a hero.

His name was Irv.

One day he was sitting behind his giant wooden desk while his students vigorously applied themselves to the task of remaining conscious while reading a vast number of pages containing the essence of Seventeenth Century English literature. Irv liked to make long assignments so as to give him the time to do what he enjoyed doing most, staring out of his window at the gradually changing seasons. It was autumn gray and cloudy. The russet leaves were working round and round his reaching mind, carrying him far out of the dismal classroom. He was far off in some soft-leaved nature bed with the auburn-haired Goddess of Autumn, Myrna, when a huge wet object covered the window.

It took him a moment to return from his dream-bliss and try to focus upon the strange thing that had just lapped across his autumnal view. His students must have assumed that the darkening of the classroom was simply the result of their steadily declining levels of consciousness. Many must have thought, one more level and I'll fall asleep and bash my head on the corner of the desk and be knocked out and roll onto the floor and get a 'C-' in English Lit.

It was a situation Irv had not encountered before, even after six years of living in the distant lands.

Utilizing all of the assertive techniques he could muster from a recent graduate course he had taken entitled, "Just Because You Are an English Teacher Doesn't Mean You Have to Be a Wimp," he strode over to the window and saw that the great dripping mass was actually the string-suspended, veined underside of a tongue.

"Class," he said as calmly as he could.

A few heads moved slightly and then returned to the hands which propped them up at appropriate angles toward the open books.

"Class!" he repeated. "Let me have your attention."

Eyes hazed by "from 'Browne's Anatomy of Melancholy'" and minds dulled by Bacon's "On Simulation and Dissimulation" stirred from the book position and assumed the lecture position. A few of the "A" students actually tilted their heads slightly and blinked.

"I hate to interrupt your reading, but there seems to be something of importance outside of our classroom. I think we should turn our attention from literature and concern ourselves with the strange object that has covered all of the large windows making up one whole wall of the room."

A lone hand rose from the rows.

"Yes, Rose. Do you have a suggestion?"

"What time is this class over? I know it's already October, but I can never remember my schedule."

"What time is class over!" he said frantically. "There is a giant tongue smeared wetly across forty

feet of windows and you want to know what time this class is over. Think about what this means. If there is a tongue that large then probably somewhere out there in our community there is a giant mouth with giant teeth and eyes and lips and ears and, worst of all, appetite."
He paced across the front of the room several times.
Another hand listlessly was raised above shoulder level.

"Yes, Thor. Can you help us?"

"Say, I think football players are supposed to get out of class five minutes before the bell to catch the football bus to the football game and the big hand is almost up to the twelve."

Irv cried out so loudly that three students raised their eyebrows, "Football! Kid, there is a tongue the size of several full grown blue whales out there and you're worrying about football."

The tongue flopped over and mountainous taste buds were exposed, some of them lumping through the open windows and protruding several inches into the class.

"Look class, the tongue is tasting our air. It wants us! The thing is hungry!"

Another hand conditioned by the protocol of a dozen years of education was elevated.

"It's time to put our books back on the shelves."

"Okay. Okay. There's nothing else I can say. Put your books back on the shelves and, when the bell rings, walk out of the building and be devoured by whatever kind of monster that thing is out there. I've done all I can do to warn you. I can only teach; I can't command."

The bell rang and 1,254 high school kids with stylish clothes and football muscles and scientific brains and dates and sex and music walked out of the school and were chewed up and swallowed by the monster.

Irv wasn't a very emotional man, but, when he heard all of the screaming and saw all the blood and

foot and arm crumbs sticking to the tongue when it returned to his window, he was somewhat disturbed.
He didn't even go to the teacher's lounge. He just sat there behind his giant wooden desk and stared at the empty room and occasionally glanced at the tongue.

"They'll never learn," Irv said as the four o'clock teacher's bell rang through the deserted corridors.

He got up from his desk, picked up his briefcase and walked through the classroom door, down the stairs, and outside the building where he was chewed up and swallowed by whatever kind of monster was out there.

It's really strange, the things that happen in far way lands.

Chapter Fifteen
Mail

I've always been one to get excited about the daily mail. I'm always looking for letters that will bring good news. Lately, alone here at the apartment, sometimes it's the fact that the mail is always waiting that gets me home. Otherwise, I might just as well sleep in the back seat of my car. It's pretty comfortable and not so damn big and filled with such sorrow. (The shower helps, but the mail is what daily draws me across the threshold here.) I look for letters from Maureen, although I really don't know what I could expect her to say anyway. I have also been waiting to hear from Amy, but, as time has slid by, it has become more and more apparent that the Earth is a solitary cell.

At school, I would check my mailbox three times a day, searching for something real. I never considered athletic lists and faculty meeting announcements a part of reality. Games and bullshit just don't have much to do with blood, food, and sex.

That's all there is to reality, you know. Blood is power, house payments, and policy. Food is bananas and emotions and sustenance for the ever-delicate ego. Sex is magnetism (gravity, salesmanship, charm, and other forces that stick us to the planet), creativity, and good ole screwing. All else is mere extension. "The Arts?" you ask. Mere Extension. You take a starving artist and he paints a pastoral scene with nice, thick, mutton walking around. You take a horny, starving artist and he paints naked women of bountiful flesh. "Philosophy?" you query. Extension only. A product of food-thick minds, using their blood-power to distract themselves from the fact that they are sexually frustrated. The Medieval, French philosopher, Peter Abelard, once expressed his worldview in the Latin phrase, Sic et Non, which, if translated honestly would state: You is gettin' it, or you ain't gettin' it. The great Greek, Socrates, probably would have been a fry cook or a plumber if it were not for the fact that his wife, Xanthippe, had the reputation of being one of the bitchiest women living the Golden Age of Athens. When he wandered barefoot about the stone plazas of the city supposedly seeking the meaning of Truth, he was actually looking for a good, five-drachma purveyor of pleasure. "But what about love?" you ask. "Does love give us power, substance, or pleasure? Is it blood, food, or sex?"

Hell, if I know. If I knew anything about love, would I be sitting here on a perfectly good Saturday morning talking to you?

So, when I rush home to fling open the mailbox downstairs in the lobby, I'm seeking something real—real words, real people, real hope. Messages from the demigods who sit out there on the edge of our disasters, sometimes sending in reinforcement and sometimes sending nothing. An unpredictable bunch. Some would even say cruel.

I've been waiting for good mail for years. Long before Maureen and Melvin's coup, I waited for letters, even when I knew they wouldn't come. Back at college I would run to the post office between classes and stare through the tiny, brass-framed window of my box at the empty space within. Sometimes a letter would slant across the view and I was always looking and thinking, it's got to be good news, change, help.

And later, married, careered, unmarried, and out of work, it's still the same.

As I said, Maureen hasn't written. The last contact I had with her was the night of the "party." The only mail I've received since her departure has been advertising, bills, and letters from Fred the Killer. At school it never varied from announcements of up-coming sporting events and faculty meetings.

When we allow the illusion of possibility to persist long after the reality of hopelessness, we can really set ourselves up for daily devastation.

It was just last night, Friday night, after being confronted by the void of junk mail and electric debts that I accepted an invitation to attend a big party at the home of educator friends.

I'll tell you about the party. I don't think I'll bother going downstairs to check the mail today.

Chapter Sixteen
The Party, or Modern Concepts of Education, or the Party

Jack Andrews had the best keg party in human history at his house trailer on the last Friday in October the year before last. He was the band teacher at Forker Middle School. I'll tell you about his party so that you'll understand about the party I went to last night. It all kind of fits together.

But first, I'll tell you about Forker Middle School, the second venue of my illustrious career as an educator. It was a new school and full of new ideas. An "open concept" school where the upstairs consisted of four, large, unpartitioned areas with an instructional media center (library) in the middle. There were over a hundred students and four teachers in each area. In terms of student-teacher ratio, twenty-five to one sounds good, but it takes on a different connotation when the fraction is left at 100 to 4.

I had transferred from the school that was the scene of "The Inquisition" and worked there the first year the school opened. There were four of us in the English Department, three women and I, and we were all going to work together so well. Martha was the head of the department. We all loved Martha because she was so much fun to have around with her enthusiastic smile and her pat on the back when times were bad. And we loved Judy because she had her hair all fixed up and she told funny stories about rape and riches. (She was a Republican.) And we loved Sandy because she was so happy to have a job she got along with everyone.

And, blush, of course, we all loved me because I was so good at running movie projectors. And, also, we all loved me because I was the loudest human being in the school and could yell, "Shut Up!" so loudly that 100-plus, screaming adolescents could hear me and would actually shut up. (Except on Fridays and the days before holidays, of course.)

The whole school talked about the English Department because we got along so well. The social studies teachers avoided interaction with students or one another by burying themselves in mountains of paper work ("Get away kid, can't you see I'm grading papers."). The math teachers openly voiced frustration with all the noise and movement. The science teachers just stayed in their storage room smoking and inventorying their stacks of new equipment. But, to the amazement and envy of all, we in English spent our open concept days encouraging one another and earnestly conversing about how Jimmy Smith and Julio Rodriguez and Elizabeth May Spackum had improved so much since school had started and how we all needed to pay close attention to Danny Dunham because his mother was a hooker and seldom home in the evenings to help him with this homework.

Martha would say, "My-oh-my, these kids can't read, write, spell, or diagram a compound-complex sentence. We have a lot of work to do but we can do it with such fine people working together. Right?"

And the rest of us would turn away modestly at the sincerity of her compliment.

The other men at school would ask me, "Watkins, how do you survive having to work with three bitches in your department?"

And I would answer, "Bitches?"

Then one Friday morning Martha started passing out Forker Junior Citizen Picture Badges to one hundred plus eighth graders right when the bell rang and also right when the principal and fourteen interested parents, school board members, and community leaders walked by on a guided tour.

Granted, her poor judgment had created the appearance and, to a certain undeniable extent, the actuality of chaos; but I was not one to criticize the actions of a beloved, fellow teacher.

During the next period Martha went downstairs to the principal, Mr. Gnu, and, according to information I later received from eavesdroppers (the office of the new school was also "open concept"), had said, "Greg is a bad teacher. It is all his fault when it gets too loud or when they can't spell. Greg is no good. Etc...."

Mr. Gnu answered, "My-oh-my, I'll have to have a talk with that fellow." He was angry but also pleased to have an offender upon whom to place the blame for the embarrassing disruption of his tour of the "school of the future."

I was called downstairs to where the principal, the assistant principal, and Theo, the administrative intern, were waiting for me in a small room. It wasn't actually a room. The only real rooms in an "open concept" school are the toilets—kudos to the geniuses of educational architecture for at least that much. This supposedly private space was created by sliding a rubber wall across one corner of the main office of the school. (It was about as private as those curtains they pull around hospital beds when they give you an enema—no one can see you but everyone on the frigging floor can hear you farting.)

"Watkins, after numerous observations, it is, unfortunately, our conclusion that you're not doing the job we've expected of you," said Mr. Gnu.

"I didn't know that," I said.

"In discussing the problem with Martha, your department chairperson, we have determined there is a lack of proper discipline in your handing of students. When over a hundred eighth-graders are walking on tables and saying dirty words, we believe it is your fault."

"Is that so?" I said. I was honestly shocked at the allegation. Martha had told me what a wonderful job I was doing almost every day. I was thinking of Martha and her perpetually sweet smile. Martha who had just that morning said to me, "Greg, I just don't know what we'd do without you in this department."

"Yes, it's true. I've noticed it myself, Watkins. Like yesterday when you were talking to that Sullivan girl. You just stood there while three students were throwing wads of paper at the trashcan. That kind of weak discipline is the basic reason for large class disturbances like the one you caused this morning. In the first place it was irresponsible of you to..."

"She was sad," I interrupted. "I was trying to cheer her up a little bit so she would feel more like paying attention when I started my lesson on dangling modifiers."

"Who?"

"Louise Sullivan, the girl I was talking to during the pre-class, paper-wad, basketball game."

"That doesn't matter. What I really want to talk about is the fiasco that occurred during my public relations tour. I find your decision to hand out Forker Junior Citizen Picture Badges right at the end of a class period on a Friday to be extremely poor judgment. Downright unprofessional."

Ozzie, the assistant principal, interjected with genuine concern emanating from the deep creases of his forehead, "Gosh, Greg, couldn't you have done it earlier in the period when you could have maintained some kind of order in the process?"

Theo started, "It was my experience as a teacher..."

"A teacher, you say?" I asked remembering what a flop he had been in the classroom where his cure-all phrase for every difficult situation was, "Hey, kid. Do you want a fat lip?"

"Er, yes. My experience as a teacher of mathematics proved to me that a well ordered, numerical approach to education is the most effective. Get down the numbers and that keeps them in line."

"Thank you, Theo," I said.

"I don't believe you're taking this seriously enough," said Mr. Gnu. "I can't allow today's embarrassment to be repeated. Martha and the other ladies in your department are endeavoring to create an atmosphere conducive to learning and apparently you are undermining that effort!"

"Now wait just a minute," I countered. "I yell 'shut up' louder than all three of them put together."

"I didn't say you were all bad, Watkins."

"I see," I said.

"I'm putting this on your personnel record and you'd better take steps to improve the situation."

And Ozzie said, "Heck, Greg, there's no reason we can't work all this out. I mean, gee, if you would just listen to Martha when she gives you her advice. Like this morning, for example, when she told you it would be unwise to hand out those identification cards at the end of the hour. If you would just listen, there will be fewer problems. Shucks, it won't be any big problem if you'd just follow a little good advice."

And then, in the futile bitterness of my premeditative, semi-subtle sarcasm, I said, "You know, I think you three gentlemen are absolutely right. As a matter of fact, I'm going to follow your advice explicitly. Why, any suggestions coming from such a master educator as Martha will never escape my attention again. No, gentlemen, I'm a changed teacher. You're the bosses and I'm the employee and it's going to be your way from here on out."

And then in unison, with smirks of satisfaction upon each of their faces, they said, "Glad to hear it, Greg."

"Cooperation is the key in the English Department," I said jubilantly.

"Well put, Greg," said Ozzie.

"Don't forget the numbers," said Theo.

"I'm sure Martha will be pleased," said Mr. Gnu.

"I'm sure she will be," I said.

"We certainly hope so," they said.

I thought about how Martha would look when I confronted her upstairs, when she would know that I knew she was a conniving, backstabbing liar. And I thought as I passed through the rubber door of the pseudo-room, these guys don't even know when someone is kissing butt.

I dashed to the staircase with the grace of a cape-less Zorro and mounted the stairs in five flying steps. With demented glare and malevolent smile, I whirled thorough the instructional media center and into the English area. "Where are you, Martha?" I grumbled to myself as I wandered the table and chair mass of students, awkward libidos, and spit wads. Aha, I figured. She must be taking a little break in the office area. "Yes, I can see you there now hiding behind a large stack of papers so you can shuffle them at the first sound of approaching administrative footsteps."

I rounded the half-wall partition.

"Greg," she said, blinking and smiling, "what was your meeting about?"

"Nothing really important, Martha. Mr. Gnu wanted me to replace you as head of the English Department, but I told him you were doing a much better job than I ever could."

That was Forker Junior Middle School, the cutting edge of progressive public education. A hot bed of intrigue and deceit. Eventually, the pressure was taken off of me when open hostility erupted between Martha and Judy over several fine points of educational philosophy, surfacing in a rather nasty encounter in which they discussed Martha's "ugly hair" and Judy's "fat legs" right in front of a Junior Great Books Club meeting. (Actually, I kind of liked Judy's legs. They were just right for holding up her not-so-bad butt. And, regarding Martha's hair, I can't say much. The only part of her I can still visualize is her smile.)

What do you say, Newfriend. Enough of these petty politics, let's get on with party #1.

The party at Jack's trailer was at the peak of all this soap opera tripe. That's why it was the best party ever. Everyone was so full of petty hatred and pent up hostility that it couldn't possibly have failed.

Let me tell you about teacher parties. I call them teacher parties because when a teacher has a party you can usually bet that almost everyone at the party will be a present, former, or future teacher.

The sequence is as follows: The teacher hangs up his trusty, yellow, dustless chalk and pale green grade book and walks down the hall saying, "Goodbye, George. Goodbye, Olive." He goes home, changes clothes, eats a light meal so he can get a buzz on faster, drives to the site of the teacher party, knocks on the door and, after being greeted by the teacher-host and/or teacher-hostess, walks through the crowded room and says, "Hello, George. Hello, Olive."

"Birds of a feather," you say? Wrong. The reason is simple. Most adults foster the same attitudes of fear and apprehension about teachers that they had throughout the years of their educational subjugation and are either hostile or uncomfortable when they are around us. They eternally imagine us as being armed with red pens and are inhibited for fear of humiliation. The arrogant doctors, dentists, and lawyers are aloof from everybody in town except other doctors and lawyers and dentists and rarely will deign to mingle with the lowly educator.

That just leaves teachers for teachers.

Which was perfect for Jack's party since it was teachers who had to confront teachers for a perfect collision that night.

Maureen and I, who were at the time experiencing a stage of our marriage somewhere on the temporal continuum between honeymoon bliss and total disillusionment, were late getting to Jack's trailer that night. We had been delayed while endeavoring to conclude an argument we had started before we left home. It ended as we pulled into the entrance to "Wally's Mobile Home Haven" with her announcement that she was going to have a horrible time at the party.

"Ya don't say," I answered in my best W.C. Fields.

She "didn't say" and we went on inside. She was wrong about the time she was going to have. After a few cups of beers, she was happily nestled in a corner talking to someone—it might have been Melvin who, though not qualifying as a teacher, was given honorary status and allowed to join the party when he offered to pay for the keg.

The good, crazy brew started working on everyone. Innuendos of honest opinion started hinting their way into conversations as guards and restraints were weakened.

"We're surprised you got through shuffling all those papers in time to come to a party," said science to social studies.

"We're surprised that you managed to wander outside of your smoking room long enough to hear the 3 o'clock bell and quit work," said social studies to science.

"How can you teach with all that god-awful noise? It would drive us crazy," said math to English.

"You mathematicians mistakenly assume silence means attention when, actually, it is more indicative of sleep. At least our students are conscious," said English to math.

Conversations became frank and there was much to be said. It's funny how much people laugh when they drink beer and tell the truth. The party was alive with people calling a bitch a bitch; a bastard a bastard. It even felt good to have someone call you a no good turd, at least that was better than all the inane platitudes that constituted ninety percent of our normal, careful conversations.

What a perfect atmosphere it was in which to open my raging heart to dear Martha. "Martha..." I started while laughing hysterically at Jack who was falling head first into a large ashtray and catching what was left of his Swede-white hair on fire, "...excuse me." I waded through the crowd to the opposite side of the room and dumped most of a cup of beer on Jack's smoldering head.

When I turned back to continue my talk with Martha, to tell her what I thought of her deceit, she was at the front door putting on her coat.

"Wait," I said halfheartedly, muted by the sounds of the party, "I've got to tell you what I think of you, Martha. I've got to tell you on this night of honesty or it will be too late because tomorrow we'll all fold right back into what we always were."

She hesitated for a moment and said something to Mr. Gnu and then turned toward me and, in a hello-party-I'm-Martha voice, she yelled above the din, "That's all right, Greg, I forgive you."

And she was gone.

At that moment I felt pain in my right butt. Something had bitten me. I turned and said to the shadowy form beneath the kitchen table, "Oh, I'll bet you're Fred the Killer, aren't you?"

And he was gone.

"I guess they all know who they are anyway," I said, losing interest in honesty.

Maureen left for the bus terminal with Melvin to pick up a canister of bull sperm for his Angus herd. Jack went outside to shorten the front porch. Mr. Gnu was nodding at me from across the room. The music throbbed at the right rhythm and everyone was moving.

At that time, I had never fooled around with other women during the years that Maureen and I had been married. But it was a night of explosions. A night of truth. I had always wanted to touch the pretty girls, no matter how much I loved Maureen and, by damn, she had left me there alone and....

I stood in the hall next to the bathroom and touched the pretty girls as they passed by.

And the pretty girls touched me and I said, "This is fun."

Then Lucy, the faculty body who for some reason was sitting on the floor of the hall closet, grabbed my leg. Mrs. Brown, the faculty large one, crashed into me and I fell into the closet right on top of Lucy. (See how innocent all this is?)

It was as if I had unleashed a separate and long suppressed stream of lust, totally unknown to me until my hand started feeling its way around the warmth of Lucy's massive right booby while she kissed me and kissed me.

She wasn't better than Maureen, probably not as good, but, by God, she was different. "Oh, no," I thought. "One kiss from another woman and I'll be a philanderer forever."

Then Maureen came back. I rolled out of the closet and stood up grinning. She didn't notice. She wasn't looking.

I think someone turned up the volume on the music because we all had to talk louder and laugh louder.

Jack was making sawing noises outside in the yard where he had pulled the wooden steps away from the doorway to shorten them.

Mr. Gnu made his way over to me through the ceaseless motion of the crowd crammed into the narrow confines of the house trailer and said he was really pleased with the way my section had improved and, also, how I was really a decent person to have apologized to Martha for not listening to her, and for telling her that I would follow her advice from then on.

I told Mr. Gnu his ass was covered with lipstick, but he didn't remember because a moment later he stepped out the front door and fell on his face because, as I said, Jack was off shortening the front porch.

There was laughter, sex, insults, great truths, and a chipped tooth (Mr. Gnu's). What can I say? It was a perfect party.

Chapter Seventeen
"Look. Look. The dogs are doing it."

It's been over two years now that people have been trying to resurrect the spirit of ire and honesty that was spontaneously generated by Jack's party.

I don't think it can happen. There are too many delicate balances, too many coincidental intersections of personality and circumstance to expect such a recurrence in one person's lifetime. Jack's quintessential party was the precise combination of just enough emotional energy generated by feelings ranging from casual irritation to outright hatred, mild acquaintance to raging lust—with just the right amount of cerebral dysfunction facilitated by a keg of Coors Beer.

I knew it was hopeless, but I kept going to the parties. My loyal friends were there, too. We usually drank more than before and got bloated and depressed, but the parties kept happening and I kept going—that is until last night's debauch. That will be the final party.

Maureen gone and spring, a melancholy mockery of ancient times of soft breezes, verdant wonders, and love—there was no immunity to the emptiness, even in meditation.

"H_ _ _!" I thought on Level #5.

The phone rang on a Friday afternoon. I knew it was Shirley and Louis having another keg party so I answered. Shirley and Louis had lived in the same house together for years. They kept separate lives and, yet, had such common interests that they had maintained a housekeeping relationship that was as strong as most marriages.

Boy, was Shirley pretty, but she had always just thought of me as being Maureen's husband.

"Hello, Shirley," I said.

"Hi, Greg," answered a sexy voice. "How'd you know it was me calling?"

"I could tell by the increase in my pulse-rate when the phone started ringing."

"Oh sure, Greg."

"How're you doin', Shirley?"

"Hey, pretty good, Greg. How about you?"

"Not bad. Ain't been gettin' any, but, other than that minor oversight, not bad."

"Poor baby," Shirley cooed.

"Say, Shirley."

"What, Greg?"

"Aren't you going to invite me to a keg party at your house tonight?"

"Oh, yeah. Do you want to come to a keg party at our house tonight?"

"What a nice idea," I said. "A party."

"So?"

"Yeah?"

"Are you coming?"

"Of course.

"Say, Shirley."

"What, Greg?"

"Why don't you say to hell with the party and come over here and ball me instead?"

"Ha, ha."

"That's what I thought."

"So, you going to come over about eight?"

"Where?"

"To the damn party Louis and I are having tonight. Jeezo-peezo, Greg, pay attention, will you?"

"Sorry. I got distracted thinking about your body."

"Try to control yourself."

"It's not easy."

"Ha, ha. You coming over?"

"Sure, Shirley. I'll be there."

Click.

Shirley and Louis always have keg parties because they love animals.

It should be easy to be on time after your wife has left you, but, somehow, you're late anyway—for different reasons.

I was late to the party because I spent over a half an hour just wandering around the apartment before leaving. I had a pattern, a path I followed from the kitchen, where I opened the refrigerator; up one step to the living room, where I touched the phone; over to the bathroom where I didn't look in the mirror; across the living room to the bedroom, where I stared at the wrinkles in the bedspread. I slowly covered the pattern several times. Each time I went through the motions a little slower, a little sadder. I was lost in my own apartment. I was looking for something but I had no clear notion of what it was because I was lost. There was some needed ingredient for the coming evening that was missing. The refrigerator? No, they had the beer. The phone? No, it would call me soon enough. The toilet? Well, maybe, but that wasn't it. The bedroom? Yes, the bedroom.

Ring.

"Hello."

"Hi, Greg. This is Fred the Killer."

"I don't know, Fred, you might be right but I'm not sure."

Click.

The bedroom. What was it?

Was I looking for Maureen? No, that wasn't it, it couldn't be. She wasn't going to the party with me.

I suddenly figured it out, the mystery of my displaced wandering.

I had been subconsciously looking for the five-pack of William Penn cigars I had left on the windowsill next to where I would stretch out on the floor. Since Maureen's departure, I don't use the bed very often and when I do, I sleep on top—never pulling down the sheets and climbing in. I don't smoke much but I like to buy cigars. The night before I had intended to lie on the floor and blow smelly smoke out the window into the fresh, spring-night air, but had decided if it wasn't safe to smoke in bed then it probably wasn't safe to smoke on rug either.

Yes, I would take my odorous smokes to the party just in case there was anyone there who would be appalled at the sight and sensation of a turd-sized cigar. A guy's got to be ready for anything, you know.

I headed out the door, checking for my keys, and, as I turned down the stairs, I heard an ancient echo of Maureen's voice saying, "I'm coming, I'm coming. I just have to find my other shoe."

Chapter Seventeen (Continued)
"...dogs..."

They lived in a fantastic house. Not in the informal sense of "wonderful or superb," but rather in the dictionary sense of "bizarre." When you walk across their front lawn you always have to hop and twist and jump to avoid falling into one of the multitude of dog burrows. By the dim glow of a street light I could see the sharp white presence of fanged teeth and wolfish eyes glaring up from the blackness of several of the earthen nests.

Every door into the house had a smaller, spring-loaded pet door cut into the bottom. Every window in the house had dangling screen flaps where the beasts hadn't bothered to use the pet doors and had lunged right on in.

As I entered the front door I made the standard Louis and Shirley joke, "Christ! You should see the size of those gophers in the front yard."

The house was a medley of smells. The smell of pretty, partying young women with their light perfumes and the sweet scent of their perspiration as they danced and exuded the wildness; the smell of popcorn; the smell of beer breathing from laughing mouths and bubbling from brimming cups; the smell of cat shit and pot coming from a back room which served as a den for illicit substance abuse as well as a nursery for scores of tiny, black kittens scurrying around like water bugs.

The ball was in full swing by the time I finally located my cigars (which, of course, I left in the car) and arrived around nine o'clock. The music throbbed and howled from the great speakers, the beer was cold and galloned out to everyone, and there was a steady procession of red-eyed people wandering in and out of the back room. In the kitchen, clustered coaches and religious people were shouting "Fuckin'-A" and "Praise the Lord" over the pulsing roar. Outside, in the dark backyard, I caught a glimpse of a couple who had fallen into one of the larger dog burrows and I could see they were laughing. The mongrel shepherds and pit bulls and the hairy and hairless no-names were all swishing in and out of the open doors and through the torn screens of the windows, careening through the legs of conversations and snarling and nipping at the random dignity of cats.

I found the plastic cups in the kitchen and, taking one from the middle of the stack to assure the virgin state of its use, made my way through the crowd of friends who said, "Hey, Greg," and strangers who said, "Nod."

I was heading out the back door when Lucy, the faculty body from Jack's party two years past, reached out from the hall closet and pulled me on in.

"Hi, Greg."

I kissed her sexy mouth and started feeling my way into her blouse and then around her left booby. "Say, Lucy. No kidding, I think this one is getting bigger," I said.

And she said, "Oh, Greg."

I wish Maureen could see me now, I thought as I stretched Lucy's massive bra cup from around her right breast and started sucking on the erectness of her thumb-sized nipple.

I rolled the sliding door closed and said, "Lucy, Lucy, let me take you."

And we boiled around the closet floor with its shoes and umbrellas and boxes of tax receipts from the past seven fiscal years, passions rising and raging, moans muffled by the dangle of overcoats, buttons exploding freedom from buttonholes, flesh touching flesh and she said, "Yes, Greg, yes. Fuck me, fuck me, fuck me...."

And I said, "Yes, yes, yes...."

"Yes," she said, "yes...but, of course we can't. What would happen if Maureen walked in here looking for the coat she left last winter?"

"Lucy," I said with giddy tears filling my thankful eyes with my wonderful news, "If you'd ever get your sweet butt out of the closet, you'd know that she ran away to Myrtle Beach with my brother Melvin (the bastard) weeks ago."

"Oh." she said.

"Yes, it's true, it's true," I said, realizing for the first time since my abandonment that I was glad she was gone. "We can fuck and fuck and fuck and nobody cares," I said as I wiggled my fingers in the hot moist nastiness within her lace panties.

"Maureen's gone?" she said.

"Nobody cares!" I said with crazed merriment.

And then, suddenly, her impassioned lips became cool, the undulations of her hips were stilled. "Well, I'd better go help Shirley with the popcorn. She never gets the butter right."

And, with rapid rearrangement of fabric and lightning fast buttoning of blouse and zipping of skirt, she was gone.

I sat on the floor of the closet for a long time with my feet sticking out the opened door into the hall, my dazed head peering out from between a hanging dress and Louis' London Fog raincoat.

"Oh, look what Greg can do with his hands," some female voice cried out and a cluster of faces crowded the closet door.

"Isn't that cute. He makes little nooses out of clothes hangers."

Eventually, I got up and wandered down the hall and out the back door to the patio where the keg was kept. I filled up my cup and downed the cold Coors. Too bad this isn't Budweiser, I thought distractedly as my hands shook from their contact with Lucy's skin.

I filled the cup again and sat down on a short wooden bench.

I sat there alone. Occasionally people would come out and fill their cups. It was the most distant edge of the party—way out on the toenails; while, at the same time, it was right next to the big, round, metallic keg-heart of the party. What an interesting relationship, I thought, as shivers of despair hurt me.

"Help!" I honestly said in good old communicative Level #1.

Shirley came out laughing and sat down next to me—close, touching. I was still shaking. God, she felt warm.

"Greg, I'm sorry about you and Maureen. I know it must be rough on you."

I looked off into the night trees and exhaled an invisible cloud of self-pity, "Yes," I nodded, the words barely distinguishable from the sigh that surrounded them.

"Are you lonely, Greg?"

I took her hand and, with the fresh gouge of Lucy's rejection raked across the un-healing gash of Maureen's rejection, all I could do was hold my sobbing breath and nod the truth of my suffering.

"There, there, Greg," she consoled.

"It's so empty, now," I uttered, fighting desperately for control.

"Is there anything I can do to help you?"

I looked deep into her eyes and squeezed her hand tighter and said, "Do you have any ideas?"

In the concentration of the moment, it seemed amazingly quiet. The party had gone a million miles away and it was just Shirley and I and the exciting cool of the spring darkness.

"I think I can give you something that might help you feel better," she said, almost in a whisper and I could hear the air forming the words upon her lips.

"I'll just bet you can," I crackled.

She glanced up at the door and then around the patio. "I don't do this for just anybody," she said as she pulled my hand and led me toward the thick darkness of the backyard.

"I know, I know," I gasped.

She sat me down on the grass in the shadow behind the redwood patio fence. "I'll be right back," she whispered and disappeared into the house.

It was a moment drawn long in anticipation of her return. When at last she reappeared, she hesitated at the edge of light and nervously asked, "You promise you won't laugh?"

I looked at the braless bumps of her hardened nipples pressed tightly against her sweater and said, "I promise, I promise. I won't laugh."

"Well, all right then," she said as she walked over to me and sat down with her magnificent, tight-jeaned butt pressed next to mine on the grass.

I sat there with my eyes swimming at her and then with a rattling sound that shattered the night she reached into a paper bag she had brought with her and said, "Here, honey, have a ripple potato chip."

Blink.

"Eat one of my potato chips, Baby, they always cheer me up."

"What?" I quivered.

"I said, 'Have a ripple potato chip.'"

"A goddamned potato chip!" I screamed. There I was, in near frenzy staring off into the oblivion of the star-cluttered sky, aroused to the point of carnal madness, and she offered me a ripple potato chip.

"Yes, Greg," she said defensively, "a goddamned ripple potato chip. They really help. When things go bad at work, or my mother writes one of her depressing letters, or one of my boyfriends has a premature ejaculation, or any of the thousands of things happen that can get a person down; I come out here with a few ripple potato chips— they're crunchier—and chew them while I think of some lively tune like 'The Stars and Stripes Forever' and before I know it I'm not upset anymore. What's the matter with you, Greg? Why are you looking like that? Hey, what are you laughing at? You said you wouldn't laugh at me, Greg. Now what are you laughing at?"

"You."

"You son of a bitch, you promised. I was only trying to help and if you're too damn smart-assed to accept my help and all you can do is laugh at me then fuck off."

She jumped up and I realized, in a flash, that hope is a tiny speck of almost non-existent essence and who was I to question its form?

"Wait, Shirley," I said leaping to my feet and running after her. "Wait! Don't go, please don't go. I didn't mean to hurt your feelings. Really, I'm sorry I laughed. Please come back."

She stopped on the second step to the back door and turned to me. "Do you mean it, Greg?"

"Yes, I mean it. I'll try it. I tell you nothing else in my life has worked out. Maybe your little potato chip is exactly what I need."

"You're not making fun of me?"

"No, Shirley, please, please, please give me a big bite of one of your ever so efficacious ripplers."

"Well, okay, but don't laugh at me again." She started back across the patio.

"I won't laugh. My God, how I need that potato chip. It might be my only hope." How dire it had all become—my life, my needs. I was deadly aware of how desperate the turns and realizations of my times had made me.

"Give it to me, Shirley, give it to me," I cried as I rushed toward her."

"Yes, Greg, yes. Take it from me," she cried.

In a second, she was face to face with me, right in the center of the patio.

With eyes deep into eyes we sat down on the concrete slab, cross-legged, lost in the lock of our gaze.

Then, like in the slow-motion shots of martial arts movies, she, frame by frame, withdrew a large, golden-white ripple potato chip from the big yellow bag and offered it to my fervid lips.

And with flowing motion I, frame by frame, with parting lips bowed toward the promise of my salvation with thankfulness in my weeping eyes.

Just then, Rocky, the mongrel shepherd crossed my misty field of vision and, frame by frame, took a licking lunge at the last chip of hope on the face of the planet and mouthed it.

Shirley sat there with a grin and her hand out holding a slobbery stump of salt and grease.

Devastated, I stared at her wet thumb and forefinger.

"Don't be discouraged, Greg. Here, I'll give you another one," she said as she rattled the bag. But the cause was lost.

"Crunch," said Rocky, chewing on my sanity.

In a split second eternally splintered from a passive life, I jumped to my feet screaming, "You lousy, goddamned mutt!" and picked up seventy-five pounds of fur and teeth and snarl and threw it far into the void of blackness that was the backyard.

"Whump," said Rocky.

Then, with a slight yelp, he rolled into one of the deeper dog holes and was gone.

Shirley was up and punching my face with the determined knuckles of her tight little fists saying, "You dog-murdering son of a bitch, you. No wonder your wife left you, you bastard."

I retreated toward the fence, covering my face with my arms so as to avoid the barrage of jabbing wrath.

So, they all stood around me, a circle of good friends—nice people, colleagues—lovers of good music, good poetry, good food, literature, nature, sex, and, unfortunately, dogs.

"These are my friends," I thought aloud, "They've come to tell me everything is going to be all right."

Several people returned from out in the darkness into which I had launched Rocky. I was still on the ground in a fetal position due to the severity of a blow that Shirley had delivered to my testicles.

"The poor thing is so frightened he won't even come out of his little hole in the ground," said pretty-friend, Female #1.

"If the dog's hurt, I'll..." said large-acquaintance, Male #1.

"Damn, Watkins. Why'd you do a dumb thing like that?" asked large-friend, Male #2.

"Yeah, Watkins. Why'd you do it? Why'd you throw the puppy?" said friends-acquaintances-passersby, Large Group #1. "Yeah, why? Yeah, why?"

I slowly got to my feet. The pain in my groin had moved from the realm of the physical to the realm of what cliché poets and country music singers call the heart.

"What's the matter, Watkins? Your old lady leave you so you gotta take out your frustrations on some innocent dog? Is that what it is? Is that what happened?" said medium-friend, Male #1.

"Fuckin'-A," said jock, Male #1.

"Fuckin'-A," said jock, Male #2.

"Fuckin'-A," said jock, Male #3.

Then they (all three of the jocks plus two of my good-friends) grabbed me and started thrusting me to and fro.

"Dog abuser!" cried the once party, now mob.

The women—the ones who once would find me in darkened places, who, with such sensuous mouths and with breasts against my arm would whisper nasty, beautiful words to me, the ones who had run their fingers playfully upon me—they were there, too, with faces raging, eyes glaring, throats snarling, and lips curling as they spat words like, "Damn you, Watkins, you cruel fellow," and, of course, "Greg, you're no good."

I am very strong. Most people don't know it but it's true. My friends know it sometimes like when they buy used pianos or move to upstairs apartments, but they forget. I became strong years ago working in St. Louis factories while going to college. I've stayed strong, as you know, by using such devices such as my anti-Herbert, Montgomery Ward's Dynamic Tension Spring Exerciser and, also, I load hay trucks for my friend Millard, the farmer.

And repeatedly the mob asked, "Why'd you do it, Watkins?" The jocks were angrily gripping my arms and uttering furious arrays of "Fuckin'-a's."

"Quiet!" someone yelled. So loudly that everyone actually did get quiet. (This guy could be a great "open-concept" teacher, too.)

125

It was Louis. It was his house, his dog, his party. No wonder everyone shut up. The grip upon me grew tighter.

It was midnight and the music was playing in the house making huge, wildly primitive, electric rock sounds that were thumping at the walls; the patio was littered with red plastic beer cups; the air had the smell of dope. Louis, a locally renowned educational psychologist with a forehead creased by deep-set wrinkles that are the awe of his profession, stood surrounded and braced by women who had wild free hair, jutting bosoms, seductive blouses, and low-cut jeans straining to contain swelling sensuality. There was sex in the air, there was violence in the air. The five or eleven remaining dogs were growling about the perimeter of the mob, the many cats were watching from the window ledges with the slow blinking eyes of stoic devils.

Then Louis with eyes that might well have witnessed God's annihilation of Gomorrah, said, "Is my doggy hurt?"

Everyone was stunned. Especially me.

Someone shut off the music. It was absolutely quiet for long seconds. Big men's feet shuffled slightly. A few hot tears escaped fast blinking pretty-eyes.

"Gosh," said the whispered voice of the party.

And then, from the crowd, with a very serious face, with slow and deliberate steps and a slightly nodding head came possibly-best-friend, Male #1.

Everybody listened.

"Can't you just say you're sorry, Greg," said Wes.

And the party breathed, "Yeah, Greg, just say you're sorry."

"Look," he continued, "we all know that you've been under a lot of pressure lately and that for the last several months you've been acting and talking kind of strangely. But, now that Maureen is gone we all understand. You've got a right to be a little strange. Doesn't he?" he asked, turning to the onlookers.

And the party said, "Sure."

"Now just say you're sorry and we'll have a beer and forget all about this whole ugly incident. I mean Rocky the dog is just a little shaken up. He'll be all right. Say you're sorry and just let it go. We'll have another beer."

"A beer. Yes, a beer," said the party. "Have a beer. Say you're sorry. Forget it, Greg. Yes, we'll forget it."

Louis walked over to me and with the jocks still gripping me tightly, he leaned between the friends I had in my face and said, "Aren't you sorry for what you did to my doggy?"

Listen, listen, thought the silent crowd.

And I laughed.

Bound by muscle-brained ball dribblers and by my supposedly good friends; encircled by startled-eyed and then wrath-eyed, monster good friends. I laughed loudly and deeply. It wasn't a malicious laugh, just deep. It was a deep, sad, heartfelt, helpless, forceful, get-off-my-ass laugh.

Then, as everyone stood, burning at my outburst, I (like Popeye with fresh spinach; Superman, free of kryptonite) thrust my arms against two of the gymnasium crowd and they went down. Then I spun and threw the third mentor of the locker room across the patio in the same general direction in which I earlier pitched Rocky, the errant cur. My friends suddenly remembered the pianos and quickly stepped away.

Eyeing the goodbye-faces of all my friends who had deserted me there for the sake of a mangy, potato-chip-stealing dog; I walked around the corner (no one spoke) of the house (no one said, "Hey, Greg, come back, to hell with the dog,") with the pack sniffing their wet noses at the seat of my pants.

I stood in the street for long moments, listening. First there were no voices, then some, then shouting and laughter, and, finally, the clear-crying words, "Look. Look. The dogs are doing it."

I sneaked to the corner and looked around to see a pair of dogs locked tightly in love.

"Get a bucket of ice water," someone said.

PART THREE

Waiting

Chapter Eighteen
"...waiting, that is."

How much of it we do in our lives, waiting, that is.
All of our lives for some of us, ay, Newfriend?
Waiting.

When we are infants, we can't wait until we are three and quit crapping our pants and disappointing our parents. Once accomplished, we pace the front sidewalks of our existences on scooters, impatient for the years to speed by and gain us entry into school. "Hey, you little fart," says Uncle Dan who drinks too much and talks dirty to the little kid, "do you get to start kindergarten this year?" "Nah, Uncle Dan," says Littlefart who idolizes gruff old Uncle Dan, "my birthday ain't 'til Janawary and so I gots to stay home 'nother year—shit."

But finally, the requisite number of months is accumulated. We are led through the towering doors of a public institution of learning where, once our confidence is won by the smiling lady who shows us a box with more Crayolas than we ever knew existed, they lock us up and throw away the key for a half dozen or so years. Eventually, after eons of waiting to get out of elementary school, we get to be junior high school kids and ache as we wait for time to make us sixteen so we can skid corners in Daddy's big automobile, or maybe even get laid in the back seat if we are precocious. "Hey, Farthead," says the bully who flunked enough grades to have the distinction of possessing the only valid operating license in the eighth grade, "when ya gettin' your license?" "Aw, fuck, shit, damn, piss," says mid-pubescent Littlefart, "not for another twenty-three and a half months—shit."

And then, with a pleasant but somewhat disquieting acceleration, years begin whirring past us and, at last, the long-awaited celebration arrives—high school graduation where the class smart kid lists appropriate clichés and the principal or superintendent tells us that all the persistence, all the waiting has finally paid off. Now, if we are willing to spend another four, six, eight years in a higher-level prison, we've got it made. "Hey, Fartness," says the class valedictorian, "what are you going to do after graduation?" "Well, Mr. Dick-torian, I thought I might get drunk." "You can't, Ass-breath. You're not twenty-one years old yet." "Shit."

And then, after a few more years of books, bullshit, or maybe just working at Burger King, we get to be the magic age of a fully enfranchised adult: 21. Now we can go down to the bars and make fools out of ourselves with the big people.

By then we have noticed that seemingly benevolent time has sped up so that the epoch of the first decade of our lives seems to have been followed by the moment of the second. Time's smooth descent from birth to dust has gathered such momentum that it turns upon us and we cry out, "Slow down! I'm not getting all this curse of dreams and expectations finished." And we're thirty and forty and....

The last wait, from the milestone of our twenty-first year to the tombstone of our last day, is the most fleeting and difficult of them all: Waiting to be.

Following countless days of milling around the work-station traps of the never-whetted appetite of a monster economy—waiting for the Fates to create the intersection of opportunity and talent that will actualize the beautiful and powerful being shoved into the back room of our beings by obligation and fear—we pass the time watching television.

There are other kinds of waiting, too. Waiting in line at a stadium bathroom at a baseball game, waiting for our number to be called at the license plate place, waiting for a phone to ring, waiting for love, and, then sitting in a dim room playing solitaire waiting for pension checks and death.

Newfriend, I've been waiting for a long time and, with the major exception of this sunny mid-morning, I still don't have the slightest idea what it is I have been awaiting. Isn't that ironic. But, yes, today I know exactly what I'm waiting for. I believe you do too.

("Well, Herr Professor, can we not deduce that life itself is a matter of waiting and, since waiting is a pain in the ass, then is not life a pain in the ass?"

"No, Sophomore. No. There's nothing wrong with your logic—but there must be something wrong with your conclusion. There must be."

"Then why are the answers so slow coming they seem to not exist at all?"

"True. The answers probably never do come. But, sometimes we allow ourselves a life while we await them."

"Do we?"

"Yes, I've read about it.")

And as for the main character in our scenario. During the invisible suffering of an unnoticed night, lost to the back corner of some nursing home, Oldfart rolled over, farted, and died.

Chapter Nineteen
Noodle

It would be wrong to infer the bitterness of my life upon the passage of all humanity, or even upon the passage of the totality of my own existence. I have known many happy occasions throughout my life and they all weren't vindictive or drunk or insane. There have been some simple and pretty times.

I won't try to distort the truth of the good times. Let them stand.

But, it truly does seem that they are over.

I really miss them.

So, I left last night's revelry of dogs and former friends at the party of Shirley and Louis and I took a walk.

I left my car parked down the street from their house and walked away.

I walked for hours thinking of many matters.

I thought about the inevitability of a ringing telephone.

Then I thought about a walk I had taken two or three years ago before I had any notion that my life was falling apart.

One afternoon, after a hard day's yelling down at the schoolhouse, instead of walking home, I walked to most of the bars in our small city.

I started at my favorite place, The Lighthouse Lounge on Main Street. I had a couple of cold drafts and talked to my friend, Hazel the barlady. Her daughter had been one of my students and, regardless of my protests that no thanks were in order, Hazel would always get me at least one beer on the house because, "...you got my little Becky through seventh grade English." We would always laugh and I would always tell her the truth about what a fine daughter she had.

I wandered on down Main Street, stopping at a couple more drinking establishments, and then a block over to a Mexican bar where I spoke Spanish with people who couldn't understand anything I said but were polite enough to laugh at my jokes. I ate a burrito smothered in green chili and drank some more beer.

I don't get drunk very often. I don't mind a little buzz, but I really don't enjoy losing control. However, some nights are just to be followed to their mysterious destinations without question. This was to be such a night.

It was getting dark. I started calling Maureen from every new tavern I entered so she wouldn't worry about me. She always said, "Be careful, Greg. I love you." There were times when she really did understand me, that Maureen.

Nice lady. And, damn it, she still is a nice lady even though she no longer waits for me.

I went to a place that had a fake jungle set up behind the bar and drank until I saw one of the stuffed monkeys change trees.

"Fresh air!" I announced.

I bought a six-pack and took to the alleyways of the night. Miles of them.

There was a light and a basketball hoop on a garage. One of my junior high students was out there shooting baskets by himself. (They're everywhere.)

"Getting drunk, Mr. Watkins?" he asked as he dribbled the ball upon the alley pavement.

"Yeah, Scott, I guess I am," I said as I set down the remnant of my bag of beers and motioned for the ball.

We started out playing a game of "Horse" and he won. So we extended it and made it a game of "Horses."

He won the game again so we made it "Horse's Asses" and after that I gave up.

"Good night, Mr. Watkins."

"Good night, Scott. Nice game."

"Thanks."

I continued walking the shadowed alleys, taking care to place my empty cans in the conveniently located trashcans and dumpsters of the houses and apartment buildings along the way.

I left the alleys and bought another six-pack. I wasn't anywhere near to being sober, but amazingly, I wasn't yet staggering or mumbling incoherently.

I walked up the long, lighted, motel-and-fast-food lined street where high school kids rode up and down in the circling parade of Friday night's weekly ritual. They smoke their dope and drink their beer and go around and round until the lights shut off at the McDonald's and the Taco Bell and the night is officially over.

I knew of a group playing folk music at one of the bars along the strip. The group consisted of a beautiful, longhaired girl with a deep and sensual voice and two real ugly guys (who also had beautiful long hair). I sat down in the back of the crowd and tried to be inconspicuous, but they were singing and playing so well that I offered them a beer out of my soggy brown sack.

They laughed.

The management didn't, so I left.

I crossed the street and, just like the kids in their shining cars, started back the way I had come, cancelling what advancement I had made heading the other direction to anywhere.

It was time to hit my last bar because soon the town would be closed down.

The drive that had sustained me subsided as I knew the end of the evening was at hand. For the first time in my eight-hour odyssey I felt myself stagger as I entered the front door into the abandonment of a "last call for alcohol" barroom.

There was a couple at the bar whom I knew and I sat down beside them. They looked at me and said, "Would you like to go home with us and have some of our chicken noodle soup?"

And I answered, "Grobabber-lapping."

We went to their place and had some soup and then they took me home. It was 3 AM.

Pretty Maureen said, "I'm glad you called me. I would have been so worried."

And I said, "Noodle!"

And, walking along the same streets and up the same narrow alleyways, I laughed about the Friday night bar trek so long ago.

"It's a little different tonight," I said out loud. "Tonight I'm staying sober and there's nobody to call."

Then I laughed darkly and said, "Or maybe there is."

I started thinking of matters that reason had kept at bay, pained remembrances filed in places locked away by the need to survive.

To the figurative rattle of dungeon keys, I unlocked all the locks.

I thought about the time this past winter when she was angry with me. She kept saying that I didn't care about her. She was wrong but all I could do was tell her, "You're wrong, Maureen, I do care about you." And, of course, that wasn't enough. The cause of the anger is of little importance. I suppose what we were doing was building up the terrible energies necessary for our own destruction. Any excuse would suffice.

She was furious and hurt and I was, to the extent of her willingness to understand, mute.

In frustration, I grasped her face between my hands to stop her accusations and to hold her close to the ineffable telling of my loving soul.

And the gloom and scowl of her anger immediately transformed into a smile.

She was smiling.

A great feeling filled me as I looked at the upturned lips of her face squeezed between my palms and I felt as though, for that instant, she might have understood me.

"You know it, don't you? You know I care." I said.

And I let go of her face and, freed from the compression of my desperate hands, her smile fell off.

And it hurt as much to recall the loving times as it did the times of misunderstanding. I thought of the night years ago when she was sitting on my lap and kissing me and how I knew at that moment I would marry her and love her forever. And it hurt to remember that night of wonderful realization.

I thought about my goddamned meditation and the terrible isolation of its truths.

I thought about Melvin and Maureen gone forever with him. Melvin would constantly be telling her how much he cared. At heart, Melvin had always been a salesman.

I was empty.

I thought about my former friends and the party and I laughed again. This time more quietly though because it was 3:30 AM and I was walking on a street of houses full of fragile sleep. I laughed like the stars laugh, with subtle shimmer and full of the naked details that fill a night.

I thought and I walked. I laughed another quiet laugh as I recalled the conversation I had with Mr. Vincent on the way out of school yesterday. "Watkins! Come in my office. I want to talk to you," he had barked as I checked my mailbox before going home. And how I had answered with simple and absolutely honest words, "No, Mr. Vincent. I think I'd rather quit than talk to you, thank you." And I did.

Everyone was gone. Walking through an empty town I knew I had lost everyone, everything. Maureen gone because I honestly felt more than I could say. Friends gone because I honestly needed more help than I knew how to ask for. Job gone because I knew the dimensions of a profession more so than its motions and could only act out of honesty.

And, in a voice that was probably too loud for the slumbering street, I summed up the result of the curse of my meditation and said, "My wife is gone, my friends are gone, my job is gone: No bullshit!"

Gone and it was so dark.

I passed a nearly deserted, all-night, Safeway supermarket. A pay phone on the wall next to the glaring entrance rang.

"Hello, Fred the Killer," I said.

"Hello, Greg," said the voice, "I'm going to smash your head with a brick, and chop your balls with a meat cleaver, and run..."

"I know, Fred."

"Oh."

"Say, Fred."

"What, Greg?"

"Why?" I asked.

There was silence on the line for a moment and then in a voice fraught with amazement he said, "You mean you really don't know?"

"Yeah. I guess I do."

"That's better, Greg. I mean it's not like you aren't asking me.

"I'm sorry, Fred. You're right. I'll see you later."

"Your place?"

"Sure."

And I hung up.

I walked on. It was very quiet. Only a few cars drove past me as I wandered the side streets listening to the absolute silence of the dozens and dozens of large and small, square sleep-boxes full of families. Talking to Fred had shut down most of my reflective masochism. I was glad of that.

I walked until ten o'clock this morning. Late enough so that the empty apartment would be filled with bright sunlight. Bright sunlight on a Saturday morning. The grand, blue-sky, mid-morning sun pouring out great, golden quadrangles of warmth through the ceiling-high windows. It's Saturday morning and, oh, the ancient rituals of this sixth day of the week—the beautiful and child-like optimism it elicits. No school. Devour the aromatic bacon and the unhurried perfection of over-easy eggs at leisured pace and then...stick guns to the back lot for war on the dented hillside—dirt-clod grenades in awkward trajectory to dusty ruin. It's Saturday morning, maybe Dad will take us fishing out where the pond-sized puddles are called lakes and are full of no-fish but we don't care. Or perhaps it's off for a family picnic with the bugs. Maybe a bike ride with buddies far beyond the street-netted town to the river woods where, through the trees, yellow-mud licked by spring floods receded, we might watch the speedboats racing and hear them roar past and then die to bee hums far down the bend. It's Saturday morning! Just a good day to breathe the leaf-smoked air from curbside piles of autumn's crisp debris smoldering along the sidewalks of tidy front lawns. Or, by God! Look outside! It snowed—a foot maybe—and on a Saturday so there'll be time for sledding the hills a hundred runs before it's all dripped away like it does out the windows of an endless school day, leaving only the slush and the mud by 3:00. Sure, it's warm enough to swim. I know the water's a little chilly, but, feel the bright radiance of May's warm sunlight upon us. There's no wind today. Damned right! We'll all jump right in. Get the leaf rakes and build mountains for diving, and get the sleds with their fine-filed runners, and, at last, the Christmas-gift mask and snorkel and jump in—deep, deep into the marvel and challenge of Saturday morning.

Sometimes Maureen and I would wake up slowly in the luxury of a Saturday morning's spill of good light. Finding what was warm and sweet of flesh beneath the night's soft blankets, I would know with her the timelessness of un-rushed touching until, invariably, the seriousness of caress would be banished by the madness of her tickling. Sometimes we would wrestle ourselves breathless on the sunny mattress, the covers kicked to the room corners, the pillows punched and battered numb upon the floor until, suddenly full and naked upon the smiling bed, we would relish the rushing excitement of each other's love until life itself was pushing the edges of sanity with pleasure. And, finally, in the harmony of our quieted laughter, gracefully, comfortably intertwined of limb and heart, we would drift back to sleep.

Ring. A roadside telephone booth.

"It's Saturday morning, Greg."

"You're telling me, Fred. Just a few more hours. Please."

"I'm not trying to hurry you."

"I know. Good-by."

And I hung up and said to the unheeding world, "Damn the sun! Damn the lie of a Saturday morning's promise."

I climbed the stairs and found the door to my apartment wide open. The place looked just as you see it now. Where once had been the clutter of cheap furniture, now there were only dents in the carpet. It had to have been Melvin. No wonder he didn't bother locking the place. There was nothing left to steal. There was a note folded and tacked to the door. I knew what it would say and really didn't want to read it.

But, of course, I did.

Dear Gregory,

I stole your wife and now I've got your red,Mediterranean couch, too.
Ha, ha.

Love,
Melvin

I laughed and laughed. I wandered the apartment laughing as a madman laughs and the emptiness reverberated, veritably echoed with the hollow howling of unfettered mirth. Melvin owns most of the gaudy, goddamned, material world. What he doesn't own of the boat-car-house-stock-and-bond trinkets of the planet, he probably has a lien on. I mean the bastard once singlehandedly repossessed the entire storm drainage and sewage system of the town of Glober, Michigan. He's got papers, deeds, bills-of-sale, mortgages, and blood-signed notes for everything from skyscrapers to a nationwide network of sanitary napkin dispensers.

He's got it all.

Why did he want my bed, my couch, my Goodwill lamps, and my water-stained coffee table?

Don't you get it, Newfriend? It's a joke. It's a Melvin Watkins' funny.

Boy, did I laugh at Melvin's humorous jab. I laughed and laughed and laughed and then I headed down to the street and captured you.

You see, up until that point it really didn't matter if anyone else in the world knew the whole story. But, somehow, this final twist—the madness of the Mediterranean couch—pushed this morning beyond mere hopelessness and desperation and into a realm of insanity and pain that I just couldn't keep to myself. I had been mentally gathering these stories for weeks and they were just what you've been hearing for the past hours, scattered recollections of a scattered life. But then came the gaping hilarity of my brother's joke, the focus of an entire existence accomplished by a sea of wall-to-wall carpet crashing upon the white, stark-cliff shore of picture-less walls. And now everything connects.

Do you see? Do you grasp that there is some kind of natural completeness to the absolute, deadly humor of these vacant rooms? We're getting close now, my friend. Very close. I've given you a sampling of the details of a life that have expanded to the point of choking the life out of me.

Do you see? I mean, isn't there something irreconcilably absolute about all this that makes it clear that my story can only have one more detail?

You've been patient waiting here with me. I appreciate your listening. And I know I've done everything I promised not to do. I know that I tend to ramble at times. But, don't you see, soon it will all be chopped away forever and, without you, all the resolute nothingness of my life will have been for just that: nothing.

Have I lost you?

Someone has got to understand how really funny the ghastly Mediterranean couch joke is in the black humor of this morning.

You look so blank, Newfriend.

You have been listening, haven't you? You have heard the whole story? All the details.

You know about my bastardly brother, the beautiful tragedy of my wife's misplaced understanding, the travesty of my profession, the shallowness of my friends.

Now, you're smiling. You are knowingly nodding sympathy and smiling comfort.

You think you understand now.

You think that my brother, my wife, my profession, and my friends have driven me to the precipice of this Saturday morning. Don't you?"

My God! You do believe these petty matters are the crux of my death wish!

You're full of it, Newfriend! You're a wonderful person and you've been hellishly kind to listen to the tortured farce of this tale. But, by damn, you are full of shit!

I told you this wasn't a soap opera, and that's what you're making of it!

I've told you about my job and about my brother and about my wife and about my friends and their copulating dogs, but I haven't told you why I can't stand it anymore. My brother is truly a joke, my wife a haunting and beautiful memory, and my friends would probably buy me a beer next week and never mention the ugly incident that alienated me from their comfort. I could find another job.

I can live with all of that.

I just can't stand the loneliness of chronically being misunderstood in my honesty.

And now I'm not sure that you know me either.

Goddamn it! Fred! Where are you, Fred? This fool doesn't understand me. I can't get to anyone now. I tell the whole thing and Newfriend sits there thinking, "What the hell's this crackpot raving about?"

Don't worry. I'll get you to the wedding reception before the bride's through dancing, before the bowl of champagne punch is sucked dry.

FRED!

PART FOUR

On Death and Fred

Chapter Twenty
"...bullshit..."

"Fred! At last, I can hear you coming up the stairs."

Do you hear him, Newfriend? He's coming. He's wearing heavy shoes and making slow, clumping sounds muffled by the carpet.

I hope you're not angry with me. I'm sorry I yelled at you. I hope you at least have sufficient understanding of the frustration of these times to forgive my outburst.

Perhaps I've asked too much of you.

You're not full of shit, my friend.

You're just human.

"Fred, I could hear you talking in the lobby and now I hear you on the stairs. Come on in. Damn the empty Earth! Let's do get it on, let's do this dire deed!"

"Hello, Gregory."

"You're really here. You really did come. It's been such a long time and now I can hardly believe it. Here you are standing in my doorway."

"Well, what'd you expect?"

"I don't know. I don't know what I expected. It's a little scary now that you've actually shown up."

"May I come in?"

"Oh, yes. There's no doubt about it, you certainly may come in."

"Thank you, Greg. Who's that?"

"Oh, that's just Newfriend—not to worry."

"As you wish."

"You know, I thought I might recognize you, but I don't. It's been years, hasn't it?"

"Yes."

"You have such, how can I say this, distinct features. I mean, I wouldn't have forgotten your face. Those mortician eyes and wax hands and porcelain teeth, I don't think I've ever seen anyone quite like you before, that's fairly certain. And, Fred, is that your famous meat cleaver and your bloody little brick I see there?"

"Come on now, Greg, you asked me up. Now don't start getting glib with me."

"I'm sorry, I'm sorry. I am being rude. Do you want me to lie down on the floor? You can probably get better leverage that way. I could drape my head over the back of a kitchen chair like on a chopping block but, as you can see, all of my handy chairs have been spirited away."

"The floor will be fine. Perhaps over here next to the door so I can make my getaway as quickly as possible."

"Sure, Fred, anything I can do to help. By the way, where's your big ugly truck?"

"Get serious, Gregory. I had to leave it parked outside. I dispense with it on inside jobs."

"That makes good sense to me."

Pretty wild looking fellow don't you think, Newfriend? I'll bet they don't even let the likes of anybody that ugly in the door down at the VFW Hall. Do they? To hell with the wedding party. Hang around here and expand your horizons.

"Fred, let me tell you this Newfriend character has been a real pal to me today, even if I did have to use a bit of supernatural coercion to assure such fine company for my final hours. I told this patient person all the details that have led to your arrival. Isn't that wonderful?"

"I suppose."

"Hey, Fred, why don't you give old Newfriend a playful little chop to assure rapt attention for the finale?"

"Oh, Greg, I'd love to, really, but not if I'm not properly asked by the afflictee. You know how I work."

"No, I'm really not sure how you do work. I know what you do and when you do it. Beyond that, I'm not clear at all on how you operate. How long have you known me, Fred? It must be years that I've been receiving your terse little memos."

"A long time, yes, a long time. You've been one of my more extended cases. It's been years since I first got the

referral on you and, of course, I went right to work—
listening to your life, monitoring your every action,
sharpening my cleaver, writing you notes..."

"What did you say about a referral?"

"Oh, it's nothing. Yes, it's true, I've known you a long
time. Years and years."

"Don't avoid my question, Fred. You said something
about me being referred to you. Now, what does that
mean?"

"Nothing. Nothing at all. Don't get excited, Greg.
These final moments can be so pleasant. Just lie back
and relax."

"Relax, hell! You want me to relax and you just
casually mention that somebody nominated me for suicide
and you won't tell me his or her name. Goddamn it, Fred,
I've been telling my friend here about how total and
complete my life package is and then you present me with
a whole new element and then pretend it doesn't exist."

"It's really..."

"NO! Now, did someone tell you about my distress? Is
that how you found me?"

"Greg, it's not ethical. I mean I have certain standards
and I try to maintain them. It's truly not fair for you to
pressure me like this."

"Ethical! Who would possibly give a hoot? You're
holding back the one detail that can absolutely tie up this
mis-felt, mis-aimed, mis-communicated life of mine and
you're holding it back. Don't tell me about 'not fair,' Fred."

"Gregory, I'd just love to tell you but..."

"What difference can it possibly make? Who's going to
tell? Newfriend probably doesn't believe any of this is
happening anyway, and, if you're half the chopper you
claim to be, I sure won't be the one to blab about
indiscretion, will I?"

"Well...."

"There you go, Fred. I can tell by the rolling of your
beady blood-clotted eyes and the wry twist to your cracked
old face that you're just itching to tell me everything you
can. Aren't you?"

"Okay, okay. But if I tell you a little, I might as well tell you the whole thing. All the particulars about your case you don't know."

"How much don't I know?"

"Just a couple of the finer details. But I must admit, they are real doozies. Are you sure you want to know all of this? It could get a bit sticky."

"Come on, Fred. Spit it out. I doubt if I could shut you up if I wanted to now."

"You already know me pretty well, don't you, Greg?"

"Well, I always say: Know thy executioner."

"Oh, I like that. 'Know thy executioner.' May I have it printed on my business cards? It has such a Biblical ring to it. Can't you just see it printed in scroll?"

"Help yourself, Fred. Now could you get on with the missing details? I'm just dying to hear them" (Get the joke, Newfriend? "Dying" to hear them.)

"Please....You can imagine all the terrible humor I have to endure in my profession."

"Yeah, (ha, ha), Fred, (ha) go ahead, I'll try to control myself."

"Promise you won't get upset with me?"

"Tell it."

"All right. To begin with, you have seen me before. Can you guess where?"

"I don't know. I think I'd remember an ugly, face like yours—especially being green and all. What ever happened to your left ear?"

"Never mind, Greg. Just think back and see if you don't remember me from your past."

"You realize I didn't see you the night you bit me on the ass at Jack's party."

"I know. It's been more recent than that."

"You'd think I could never forget those creepy features of yours."

"Give up?"

"Hell yes, I give up. What is this, some kind of a parlor game?"

"Do you want a hint?"

150

"Sure. I'd like a hint. You know, I didn't realize the extent of the service you would provide. Not only are you an expert executioner but also a damn fine suicide social director."

"I was wearing a disguise when you saw me."

"A disguise?"

"Yes."

"Say, Fred."

"What?"

"How in blazes do you expect me to remember you if you were wearing a disguise the only time in my increasingly unfortunate life, prior to today, that I ever had the dubious pleasure of viewing you?"

"I don't. (Get it, New-what's-your-name. Get it? It's a joke. How could he recognize me if I was wearing a disguise when he saw me before?) Get it? Ha, ha."

"Jeez, Fred. Why don't you just go ahead and chop me up. I've suffered enough already."

"Okay, okay. I'll get on with my devious little tale. It's so good I've been wanting to tell someone for months but you're probably the only person who can fully appreciate the brilliance of it all. I'm certainly glad you forced me to tell you this. "You see, business was slow last winter. The Christmas rush was over and not much was happening, there's always such a slump around February. I'd been carrying you on my records for so long, I decided it was time that I prompt you a bit. You know, help you along—speed up the process, so to speak."

"A disguise, you say?"

"Yes, I'm sure you'll remember me if I put it on. I've got it in my valise out in the hall. I'll just be a moment. You'll love this, I know you will."

What do you think of this guy, Newfriend? He's taking off his clothes right out in the middle of the hall. (I hope my little-old-lady neighbor isn't watching. She doesn't shock easily, but, my God, look at those knees.) And now he's putting on some kind of face paint.

"Now promise you won't get mad, Greg. All I did was to expedite an inevitable development. You would have requested my services in the long run. I'm sure."

"I don't anger too easily anymore. I've been meditating, you know."

"Oh, yes, I do. There, I'm ready."

"Get on in here."

"Well, what do you think?"

"Oh no! Of course I know you. How could I ever forget the shroud, the white-face, the gray wig?"

"I thought you might recollect this costume."

"Is that a crossbow I see sticking out of your robe?"

"Bingo!"

"You dirty bastard."

"Now, now, Greg. Don't be short with me. It wasn't just my doing. You were well into the process of separating yourself from the everyday world anyway. I just sped it up a bit. And what better way to hasten a client's progress than to encourage the destruction of his marriage, friendships, and security? And, furthermore, what better way to facilitate such destruction than to inhibit his faculty for manipulating the truth?"

"Oh, you are a brilliant one, Fred. I'd kill you if you weren't my only way out of this despicable world. You bloody murderer."

"Don't start calling me foul names. You're the one who needs me. Remember that."

"I know it. Perhaps I should call you 'Finalfriend.' I know it now more than ever. You mean this obsession, this driving need I've developed to communicate on a real level is just some gimmick contrived by you so you can get your meat cleaver jollies?"

"Not at all, Gregory. Quite the opposite is true. I only acted within the framework of your existing meditation. I didn't create it. Your conclusions are astute; I only forced you to face the painful implications of honest communication."

"Really?"

"Oh, yes. It's very simple. The process of your enlightenment had brought you to a point where you saw through other people's self-deception and triviality. However, for the illusion of a sense of community—a sense of mutuality with the conscious world—you hung on to the ability to mask your awareness by continuing the surface word-games. And, as you well know, that's how you mortal fools live. Your society, your friends, your loves—all based on word games, white lies...bullshit, if you will. Take it away and there is nothing left. And that is what you and I did to you—you did it internally and I made you do it externally. You were well on your way when I stepped in to move things along. If you don't believe me, just ask your wife, or should I say *former wife*?"

"Nothing left at all."

"That's all that is left: nothing. You can't exist in a void, Greg. It's just too lonely. So, now you find it impossible to live any longer."

"Oh."

"And there are no exceptions. It's bullshit or the world is empty."

"No exceptions?"

"I sure don't know of any. Look at what's left of your life. Do you know any exceptions?"

"No exceptions."

"You were going to lie down over here next to the front door. Are you ready?"

"Sure."

"Oh, Good. You know, I love to help people. I love it. I love it. Let me help you now."

"Don't work up too much of a sweat, Fred. I don't want to go out feeling like some kind of a pervert."

"Just lie down and leave the rest to me."

"Hey, Fred. Maybe I'll be a star now."

"You really are distraught. You think that dead people go to Hollywood."

"Not that kind of a star. I mean a real star. You know, a heavenly body. An extra dot in the contrivance of some constellation. Stars are all alone, isolated from the touch of any other entity and yet glowing to the whole universe. Maybe I'll be a star. I feel like one already."

"I'm sure you'll be a star, Gregory. Now, please, lie down so I can have my way with you. I love it, I love it, I love it."

He loves it, Newfriend. Say, if the sight of blood troubles you, it's all right if you look the other way. I brought you up here for enlightenment not nausea.

"Don't bother talking to what's-its-name over there. People don't understand you anyway."

"I suppose you're right. I kind of like Newfriend, though. It seems like we've been through so much together this morning."

"Bullshit."

"Oh, well."

"That's my man."

"On with it!"

"Yes, yes, yes."

"But one last thing, Fred, before we finish this. You did mention that someone had referred me to you."

"Oh, that was really nothing."

"Cut the crap."

"All right. Actually, most of my cases are the result of referrals. One suffering human being attempting to help another suffering human being by passing his or her name along to me in hopes that such a friend or loved one might be served in the same tasteful and effective manner."

"How touching. Someone out there is about to have loved me to death."

"It is touching. Is there anyone you'd like to tell me about?"

"I don't know. Maybe old Newfriend over there is a prime candidate for a bit of a brick whacking."

"Get serious, Greg. This is hardly a joking matter. I take my work quite seriously. I pride myself in facilitating a dignified exit for those for whom this earthy realm has become unbearable."

"You call a meat cleaver, a brick, and a big ugly truck 'dignified?'"

154

"Well, damn, I don't charge anything for this. The least I can do is have a little fun while I'm at it."

"At least."

"Do you want to refer anyone?"

"No."

"Very well, then. Would you please lie down?"

"Who was it?"

"Who? Oh, your advocate."

"Yeah."

"Well, as I said, the party is another one of my customers. Another stubborn case, too. This person has held on longer than you have, but I've even got more confidence in this one than I ever did in you, Gregory. You people and your adherence to brittle values. It sure does slow the process up sometimes. The two of you have persisted for years. It must be in the blood."

"Blood?"

"Yes, blood."

"Melvin!"

"Who else?"

"I can understand the bastard turning me in—just another funny joke—but Melvin, my rich, materialistic, wife-stealing brother, needs your services?"

"More than most I've known and, believe me, I've been at this business for quite some time."

What do you think of that, Newfriend? Melvin and the chopper-man.

That might be the saddest part of all this. With all his wealth and insensitivity, if he's so miserable as to be on speaking terms with Fred the Killer, no wonder there is such desperation among the good and honest people of the world.

"Chop to your horny, fucking, heart's content, Frederick. Get on with it!"

"Right!"

"Now!"

"I will, I will, I will. Oh, golly, how I love my work. But, there is one other thing."

155

"What now, Fred? Let me guess. Maureen's your mistress. Right?"

"Oh, no, no. She had nothing to do with any of this."

"Then why the delay?"

"On the way up here I ran into the mailman and told him I would bring your mail up to you. Just a tidy little detail I need to complete. I've got it in my jacket pocket out in the hall. I'll get it for you."

"How considerate."

"Well, I did promise and I am a fiend of my word. You do want to look at it, don't you?"

"Such integrity. No, to hell with the mail. I've spent my life waiting for it and all that ever comes is a bunch of computer-licked bills and sales catalogues."

"Not to be nosy, but I did notice one envelope that looked like personal mail."

"Give it to me!"

"No need to grab."

Listen to this, Newfriend. Listen to the beautiful words. Feel how they flow into the vacancy of my heart.

Dear Greg,

I do understand. I think of you so often. We walked around the duck pond together at the English teachers' convention. My name is Amy. I'm sorry I have taken so long to reply to the question in your note, but this is new for me—feeling so much for someone I will only know for a half an hour. I love you, Greg.

I know I am safe in telling you.

I'm going to be married very soon, you're already married, it doesn't matter. The way I love you is unique. It dwells apart and contradicts nothing of the rest of my life.

I love you because, while you were making me laugh by telling me about the insuperable arrogance of the hotel ducks, I heard a silent goodness in your being that still speaks within me.

And, though, likely, I will never see you again, I will always know that you care. I will always carry with me the stillness and beauty you silently spoke to me in our thirty, eternal minutes together.

You are a loving person, Greg.

I heard you. I really heard you.

I love you, Greg.

Goodbye.
Amy

Isn't that beautiful. She heard me, Newfriend.

My God, I do have a voice and it has been heard!

"Why are you looking like that, Greg? What was in that letter? You're smiling! There's no world left for you, there's no place in the world for truth, Greg. There's no reason to smile. Laugh hysterically, yes, but you can't smile. Gregory, you're a pathetically isolated and empty man. How can you be smiling?"

"So long, Fred."

"What do you mean? No! It's too late! I'm here and I'll have my joy. You can't turn back now—we've gone too far. I'm here. Forget my escape. I'm locking the door!"

Slam. Lock.

He's coming at me with that damned meat cleaver. You can't help me, Newfriend. You're real; I'm fictional. Thanks for nothing anyway.

"I don't need you anymore, Fred. Put down that meat cleaver before someone gets hurt."

"I'm going to chop..."

"I know, I know. I've read your letters and answered your calls. You were wrong. You are wrong. It was only a moment and maybe never again, but now I know it can happen. This letters says "...Greg, I heard you...." It proves I'm not alone. It proves the world lives and, bless the lovely truth of Amy: I live in the world!"

"That's nothing. I've been hearing you for years. What else is new?"

"Everything. You've been listening but you're the end of communication; this is the beginning!"

"Now I'm starting to see...this letter, it was from some woman. Wasn't it? Sure it was. You animal, you're willing to defy my truth for a piece of ass. Gregory, you really disappoint me. I thought you understood how artificial and transitory your entire old world was. You'll just get your rocks off and be more miserable than you ever were."

"I'll never see her again, Fred. I would never try to find her. Our time is complete."

"What was it she said, 'I heard you, Greg.' Oh, you fool, how you deceive yourself. You make me laugh."

"You're wrong this time, Fred. I'm incapable of self-deceit. Remember? You made damned certain of that. No, my little green buddy, it turns out that there is an exception. There are real moments, real connections possible in this life. I know the possibilities of their intersecting are remote, but, you're wrong, such possibilities do exist. I know it happened once. Here, you read the letter. You'll see I'm right."

"Letter-smetter. Go to hell. Greg, you're no good."

"Goodbye, Fred."

"Bosh! There is no way that I'm going to leave here without my action. I need my action and I'll have it. Do you hear me? I'll have my action!"

"But I want to live, now."

"Too late, Greg. I'm getting really impatient with you. Do you think you're the only cop-out creature I have to service today?"

"Listen, Fred. I don't want to be dead. I feel like there's a reason to live."

"I don't care, you Indian-giver. I mean, you ask a guy up to your apartment, talk real nice, say you'll cooperate, and then just turn right around and tell him 'NO.' You're a no-good teaser, you are, and I'm going to chop..."

I think he means it, Newfriend. As you can see, he is going into some kind of Mish-Kia spin. There might be no surviving this. It could really get messy.

"Watch it, Fred! You almost hit me."

"Don't I know it, you nasty old gimme-back."

He's pretty good at this, you know it? I think he'll probably kill me soon if I don't think of something clever— or should I say "cleaver?" Ha, ha.

"Fred! That was close."

"Stand still, curse you. Nobody plays games with Fred the Killer."

Swish.

I've got to think of something. You know, I've heard that sometimes..."Yikes! Close again."

"Die, fool, die!"

...severed nerves have been known to regenerate...perhaps there's still a little bullshit left in the old cranium....

...and from my neck so free
The albatross fell off, and sank
like lead into the sea...

"Hold on, Fred. Stop for a minute. Not like this. Please, not like this."

"You asked for it, Greg. Winner takes all the marbles here, you know!"

"Now, Fred, no need to get so harsh."

"Why not?"

"Wait, I've just gotten too emotional about this whole thing. You're probably right. Amy's just another physical whim, a piece of ass as you put it, and that's just a bunch of grunting and moaning, no real communication there. Hell, she might not even be on the pill."

"That's right, Greg. We're not dealing with moments here. We're dealing with souls."

"Well put. I like that—dealing with souls. Not bad."

"Thank you. This is more like it. I'm your friend, Greg. I've come to help you."

"And I've been cruel. It is cruel to lead someone on for years and then shut them down right at the last second."

"It's not very easy to take, I'll assure you. You've really gotten me worked up."

"I have been treating you poorly. After all, I did invite you up. Didn't I?"

"You didn't have to answer the phone. You could have thrown my letters away."

"Yes, I know. And you've been very patient with me. You must be quite busy now that it's May and so many must be dealing with the disillusionment of spring."

"If you only knew."

"And, after putting you through all of this complication, I fear I might seem presumptuous to ask one final favor of you. A last request, if you would."

"What is it, Gregory? This has not been easy. I don't like to sweat."

"Well, I've gotten so worked up here in the last few minutes. I don't want to die this way with adrenalin pumping through my veins. I don't feel very serene at all. I think if I could have just one last beer before I go, it would be much more peaceful at the end."

"Greg, I don't have all day."

"Just one can of Budweiser before I confront the great mystery of death."

"Well, if you put it that way...only one beer and then you'll cooperate?"

"One beer...trust me. You know I'm a perfectly honest man."

"Hurry up."

"Thank you, Fred. Now if you'll just lower that meat cleaver you have aimed at my body, I'll reach into the refrigerator here and get myself a cool one."

"I'll just keep my meat cleaver ready for action, thank you."

"I'm sure you will, old buddy. I'm sure you will."

The grip of this pistol is very cold. I'm certain the bullet is bitterly cold as well.

Clunk!

Did you hear that, Newfriend?

The sound of a meat cleaver hitting the floor, dropped from a now non-existent green hand. A fine, sharp meat cleaver left by the disappeared Fred.

And the gun? The gun is now a forty-five caliber, semi-automatic, gas-operated honeydew melon.

If I were real, you could share this with me.

So good of Fred to leave his cleaver for me. I'll chop my melon open with it.

Chop!

It's full of life and the warmth and promise of a sunny, spring, Saturday morning.

It will taste so good.

Other Works by Robert Nichols

Most of these titles are currently published as e-Books available through all the major distributors—Kindle, Nook, etc.
Also, printed editions are in process as books-on-demand, I will get them out—hey, it's a lot of work.

Books etc.

The Kristin Book (1987)

Story of the first fifteen years of the life of my daughter who was born with Down Syndrome.
This book, reissued with an update, is now available in eBook format as *The Kristin Book: Update 2013*

Take the Aspen Train (1988)

Co-authored with Edward Larsh. Coffee table, Colorado history / social philosophy / train book. *(No longer available.)*

Adventures in the High Wind (1990)

Collection of my poems, stories, and essays.
eBook edition, 2013.

Leadville, U.S.A (1993)

Co-authored with Edward Larsh. Oral history of Leadville, Colorado. *(No longer available.)*

The High Priest of Hallelujah (1999)

Niche-less novel of poetic vision, humor, and satire.
eBook edition, 2015.

Summer Words, 2000 (2001)

Collection of short essays about laughter, God, knife throwing and much more.
e-Book edition, 2014.

The Booklets (2001 and...)

12-14 page booklets of poetry, short stories, essays—you know: literature. Currently there are five of these little gems published with more to come. Some day...

The Five Great Truths of Uncle Bob (2002)

A culminating work of philosophy, religion, and practical wisdom (and all on one side of a sheet of paper).

God of the Poets (2003)

It took me twenty years to get this one right. When I finished the first version in '83 I didn't know enough to write my own novel. Perhaps now I do. I was pretty much just a stenographer for the real author, God. This isn't traditional stuff. It's a story of art, love, humanity and... *the purpose of life.*
e-Book edition, 2014.

Albatross: The Curse of Honesty (2013)

The first novel I wrote, and re-wrote, and finally published. It's a funny and touching tale of a fellow whose life is nearly destoyed by the curse of absolute honesty.

The Great Book of Bob (2009)
The Great Book of Bob eBook edition (2014)

A unified collection of humorous, soul-wrenching, and harshly honest tales and thoughts gleaned from a lifelong love story— stories of a poet's love of sunrises, poetic epiphanies, laughter, and for the soulmate of his life. And the best part about it, it's not some icky-sticky, lovey-poo bunch of hearts and flowers. It's hard-edged wonder and real reason for all of us to be glad to be alive. I tell *my* stories that we may each realize the significance of our own.

Uncle Bob's Big Book of Happy (2017)

I should make this clear from the start. None of this is easy. The first chapter of this work starts out saying exactly that: This will not be easy. I tell some hard truths. Don't be misled by the mirthful lilt of my title. Uncle Bob here will do his best to help you be happy, but none of this means diddly-squat if you can't face harsher aspects of our everyday journey. I write this book in hopes that my stories, theories, blathering bilge and sublime prayers may be of help to you in avoiding the burden, the curse of bitterness. It's no fun living in a world of bitchy whiners, angry jerks, and cranky bastards. You know what I mean.

THE FOOTLOCKER SERIES

This is a series of eBooks gleaned from fifty years of writing excavated from Robert Nichols' old footlocker of notebooks and scraps of papers—the repository of a life of art.

For information contact Robert Nichols at Mtmuse44@aol.com.

Titles:

about Time
about Mountain Living
about Seasons
about Paths

about Time: Poems and Other Stories (2015)

The first in the series—poetry, stories, and photography about ancient time, the time of children, the time of young adults, and the time of growing old. It's really not about time at all. This is a book about life.

about Mountain Living: Finding a Way *(2015)*

A journey told in story and poem. A life trek from discontent and restlessness to commitment and discovery. This work tells of a succession of habitats and lifestyles progressing farther and farther from the city and further into a better destiny—from apartment to cabin to tipi to hilltop shrine of art, nature, and spirit. A journey from complacent certainty to out-on-the-edge primal survival. Perhaps my story will encourage yours. And, beyond the tale I tell, just read the poems and stories as the art they are intended to be. You will laugh and weep and contemplate—you will be changed.

about Seasons: the Wind and Weather of Our Days (2016)

Poems of the seasons—not just some cliché sweetness about leaves and blossoms either. This is the core stuff of being. Seasons, wind, and weather—the fierce and beautiful power of Nature that can keep us humble and exhilarated throughout our lives. It is the very "life and death" intensity of these metamorphic cycles that excites the turning of our years with risk and wonder. Time takes away our days, storms wash away our safety, seasons etch our flesh with danger. Old Spirits out on the plains once told me, "Earth shall never be tame... celebrate your fear and feel you are alive!" Yes!

about Paths—Journeys Through Wonder, Danger, and Self

The fourth in the Footlocker Series of books published by Robert Nichols, about Paths is another collection of beautiful and moving poetry and thought-provoking essays. Robert artfully takes you with him as he recounts youthful journeys hitchhiking the country, expresses vignette word-sketches of people and places along the way throughout the years, and gives a sense of purpose to the paths all of us take. Read these works and you will know the harsh and enlightening truths of the road, you will contemplate the ugly realities of American racism, you will observe the humor and pathos of the passing scene—you will travel the path of an open-hearted poet.

Robert Nichols writes, carves, sings
and loves life in Oregon.

www.ingramcontent.com/pod-product-compliance
Lightning Source LLC
Chambersburg PA
CBHW060224180626
46813CB00007B/2947